We Must Love Someone

Ruskin Bond is known for his signature simplistic and witty writing style. He is the author of several bestselling short stories, novellas, collections, essays and children's books; and has contributed a number of poems and articles to various magazines and anthologies. At the age of twenty-three, he won the prestigious John Llewellyn Rhys Prize for his first novel, *The Room on the Roof*. He was also the recipient of the Padma Shri in 1999, Lifetime Achievement Award by the Delhi Government in 2012 and the Padma Bhushan in 2014.

Born in 1934, Ruskin Bond grew up in Jamnagar, Shimla, New Delhi and Dehradun. Apart from three years in the UK, he has spent all his life in India, and now lives in Landour, Mussoorie, with his adopted family.

RUSKIN BOND

We Must Love Someone

RUPA

Published by
Rupa Publications India Pvt. Ltd 2023
7/16, Ansari Road, Daryaganj
New Delhi 110002

Sales centres:
Prayagraj Bengaluru Chennai
Hyderabad Jaipur Kathmandu
Kolkata Mumbai

Copyright © Ruskin Bond 2023

This is a work of fiction. Names, characters, places and incidents are either the product of the author's imagination or are used fictitiously and any resemblance to any actual person, living or dead, events or locales is entirely coincidental.

All rights reserved.
No part of this publication may be reproduced, transmitted, or stored in a retrieval system, in any form or by any means, electronic, mechanical, photocopying, recording or otherwise, without the prior permission of the publisher.

P-ISBN: 978-93-5702-529-4
E-ISBN: 978-93-5702-530-0

First impression 2023

10 9 8 7 6 5 4 3 2 1

The moral right of the author has been asserted.

This book is sold subject to the condition that it shall not, by way of trade or otherwise, be lent, resold, hired out, or otherwise circulated, without the publisher's prior consent, in any form of binding or cover other than that in which it is published.

CONTENTS

Introduction — *vii*

1. We Must Love Someone — 1
2. A Love of Long Ago — 2
3. Binya Passes By — 8
4. The Story of Madhu — 20
5. Who Kissed Me in the Dark? — 25
6. The Girl on the Train — 31
7. His Neighbour's Wife — 35
8. Calypso Christmas — 41
9. The Garlands on His Brow — 46
10. The Woman on Platform No. 8 — 52
11. Mrs Roberts — 58
12. From Small Beginnings — 63
13. The Last Tonga Ride — 76
14. The Crooked Tree — 91

INTRODUCTION

When we think of 'love', our mind usually goes to stories of Romeo and Juliet or Laila and Majnu. These are great tales of romance and tragedy, immortalized through the ages. But love is vaster than that—it is the first sight of snow-covered mountains when the sun is setting. Love lurks in a mother's lullaby, a dog's wagging tail, a stranger's smile, the waterfall-like rustle of deodars... The warmth and fondness we feel in these moments is what makes life beautiful.

In *We Must Love Someone*, I wish to explore the many dimensions of love. There are tales of love for friends, like 'Calypso Christmas', and of getting through hard times, like 'The Crooked Tree'. Stories like 'The Woman on Platform No. 8' speak of a mother's love towards a child that is not hers. And there are, of course, stories about romantic love, like 'His Neighbour's Wife', and its loss, like 'A Love of Long Ago'. Other stories, like 'The Story of Madhu' and 'The Girl on the Train', are about encounters with strangers who have managed spark something that I would call love.

I hope this book about love, in all its shapes and sizes, full of affection towards strangers, friends, lovers and animals,

We Must Love Someone

manages to bring some hope and joy into your lives. After all:

Without the touch of love
There is no life, and we must fade away.

Ruskin Bond

WE MUST LOVE SOMEONE

We Must Love Someone
If we are to justify
Our presence on this earth.
We must keep loving all our days,
Someone, anyone, anywhere
Outside our selves;
For even the sarus crane
Will grieve over its lost companion,
And the seal its mate.
Somewhere in life
There must be someone
To take your hand
And share the torrid day.
Without the touch of love
There is no life, and we must fade away.

A LOVE OF LONG AGO

Last week, as the taxi took me to Delhi, I passed through the small town in the foothills where I had lived as a young man.

Well, it's the only road to Delhi and one must go that way, but I seldom travel beyond the foothills. As the years go by, my visits to the city—any city—are few and far between. But whenever I am on that road, I look out of the window of my bus or taxi, to catch a glimpse of the first-floor balcony where a row of potted plants lend colour to an old and decrepit building. Ferns, a palm, a few bright marigolds, zinnias, and nasturtiums—they made that balcony stand out from others; it was impossible to miss it.

But last week, when I looked out of the taxi window, the balcony garden had gone. A few broken pots remained, but the ferns had crumpled into dust, the palm had turned brown and yellow, and of the flowers nothing remained.

All these years I had taken that balcony garden for granted, and now it had gone. It jerked me upright in my seat. I looked back at the building for signs of life, but saw none. The taxi sped on. On my way back, I decided, I would look again. But it was as though a part of my life had come to an abrupt end, a part that I had almost come to take for granted. The link between youth and middle age, the bridge that spanned that gap, had suddenly been swept away.

And what had happened to Kamla, I wondered. Kamla, who had tended those plants all these years, knowing I would be looking out for them even though I might not see her, even though she might never see me.

Chance gives, and takes away, and gives again. But I would have to look elsewhere now for the memories of my love, my young love, the girl who came into my life for a few blissful weeks and then went out of it for the remainder of our lives.

Was it almost thirty years ago that it all happened? How old was I then? Twenty-two at the most! And Kamla could not have been more than seventeen.

She had a laughing face, mischievous, always ready to break into a smile or peals of laughter. Sparkling brown eyes. How can I ever forget those eyes? Peeping at me from behind a window curtain, following me as I climbed the steps to my room—the room that was separated from her quarters by a narrow wooden landing that creaked loudly if I tried to move quietly across it. The trick was to dash across, as she did so neatly on her butterfly feet.

She was always on the move—flitting about on the verandah, running errands of no consequence, dancing on the steps, singing on the rooftop as she hung out the family washing. Only once was she still. That was when we met on the steps in the dark, and I stole a kiss, a sweet phantom kiss. She was very still then, very close, a butterfly drawing out nectar, and then she broke away from me and ran away laughing.

'What is your work?' she asked me one day.

'I write stories.'

'Will you write one about me?'

'Some day.'

I was living in a room above Moti-Bibi's grocery shop near the cinema. At night I could hear the soundtrack from the films. The songs did not help me much with my writing, nor with my affair, for Kamla could not come out at night. We met in the afternoons when the whole town took a siesta and expected us to do the same. Kamla had a young brother who worked for Moti-Bibi (a widow who was also my landlady), and it was through the boy that I had first met Kamla.

Moti-Bibi always sent me a glass of kanji or sugarcane juice or lime juice (depending on the season) around noon. Usually the boy brought me the drink, but one day I looked up from my typewriter to see what at first I thought was an apparition hovering over me. She seemed to shimmer before me in the hot sunlight that came slashing through the open door. I looked up into her face and our eyes met over the rim of the glass. I forgot to take it from her.

What I liked about her was her smile. It dropped over her face slowly, like sunshine moving over brown hills. She seemed to give out some of the glow that was in her face. I felt it pour over me. And this golden feeling did not pass when she left the room. That was how I knew she was going to mean something special to me.

They were poor, but in time I was to realize that I was even poorer. When I discovered that plans were afoot to marry her to a widower of forty, I plucked up enough courage to declare that I would marry her myself. But my youth was no consideration. The widower had land and a generous gift of money for Kamla's parents. Not only was this offer attractive; it was customary. What had I to offer? A small rented room, a typewriter and a precarious income of two to three hundred rupees a month from freelancing. I told the brother that I would be famous one day, that I would be rich, that I would be writing bestsellers! He did not believe me. And who can blame him? I never did write bestsellers or become rich. Nor did I have parents or relatives to speak on my behalf.

I thought of running away with Kamla. When I mentioned it to her, her eyes lit up. She thought it would be great fun. Women in love can be more reckless than men! But I had read too many stories about runaway marriages ending in disaster, and I lacked the courage to go through with such an adventure. I must have known instinctively that it would not work. Where would we go, and how would we live? There would be no home to crawl back to, for either of us.

Had I loved more passionately, more fiercely, I might have felt compelled to elope with Kamla, regardless of the consequences. But it never became an intense relationship. We had so few moments together. Always stolen moments—on the stairs, on the roof, in the deserted junkyard behind the shops. She seemed to enjoy every moment of this secret affair. I fretted and longed for something more permanent. Her responses, so sweet and generous, only made my longing greater. But she seemed content with the immediate moment and what it offered.

And so the marriage took place, and she did not appear to be too dismayed about her future. But before she left for her husband's house, she asked me for some of the plants that I had owned and nourished on my small balcony.

'Take them all,' I said. 'I am leaving, anyway.'

'Where are you going?'

'To Delhi—to find work. But I shall come this way sometimes.'

'My husband's house is on the Delhi road. You will pass that way. I will keep these flowers where you can see them.'

We did not touch each other in parting. Her brother came and collected the plants. Only the cacti remained. Not a lover's plant, the cactus! I gave the cacti to my landlady and went to live in Delhi.

◆

And whenever I passed through the old place, summer or winter, I looked out of the window of my bus or taxi and saw the garden flourishing on Kamla's balcony; leaf and fern abounded, and the flowers grew rampant on the sunny ledge.

Once I saw her, leaning over the balcony railing. I stopped the taxi and waved to her. She waved back, smiling like the sun breaking through clouds. She called to me to come up, but I said I would come another time. I never did visit her home, and I never saw her husband. Her parents had gone back to their village, her brother had vanished into the great grey spaces of India.

In recent years, after leaving Delhi and making my home in the hills, I have passed through the town less often, but the flowers have always been there, bright and glowing in their increasingly shabby surroundings. Except on this last journey of mine...

And on the return trip, only yesterday, I looked again, but the house was empty and desolate. I got out of the car and looked up at the balcony and called Kamla's name—called it after so many years—but there was no answer.

I asked questions in the locality. The old man had died, his wife had gone away, probably to her village. There had been no children. Would she return? No one could say. The house had been sold; it would be pulled down to make way for a block of flats.

I glanced once more at the deserted balcony, the withered, drooping plants. A butterfly flitted about the railing, looking in vain for a flower on which to alight. It settled briefly on my hand, before opening its wings and fluttering away into the blue.

BINYA PASSES BY

While I was walking home one day, along the path through the pines, I heard a girl singing.

It was summer in the hills, and the trees were in new leaf. The walnuts and cherries were just beginning to form between the leaves.

The wind was still, and the trees were hushed, and the song came to me clearly, but it was not the words—which I could not follow—or the rise and fall of the melody which held me in thrall, but the voice itself, which was a young and tender voice.

I left the path and scrambled down the slope, slipping on fallen pine needles. But when I came to the bottom of the slope, the singing had stopped and no one was there. 'I'm sure I heard someone singing,' I said to myself, but I may have been wrong. In the hills it is always possible to be wrong.

So I walked on home, and presently I heard another song, but this time it was the whistling thrush rendering a broken melody, singing of dark, sweet secrets in the depths of the forest.

I had little to sing about myself, as the electricity bill hadn't been paid, and there was nothing in the bank, and my second novel had just been turned down by another publisher. Still, it was summer, and men and animals were drowsy, and so too were my creditors. The distant mountains loomed purple in the shimmering dust-haze.

I walked through the pines again, but I did not hear the singing. And then for a week I did not leave the cottage, as the novel had to be rewritten, and I worked hard at it, pausing only to eat and sleep and take note of the leaves turning a darker green.

The window opened on to the forest. Trees reached up to the window. Oak, maple, walnut. Higher up the hill, the pines started, and further on, armies of deodars marched over the mountains. And the mountains rose higher, and the trees grew stunted until they finally disappeared and only the black spirit-haunted rocks rose up to meet the everlasting snows. Those peaks cradled the sky. I could not see them from my windows. But on clear mornings they could be seen from the pass on the Tehri road.

There was a stream at the bottom of the hill. One morning, quite early, I went down to the stream, and using the boulders as stepping stones, moved downstream for about half a mile. Then I lay down to rest on a flat rock, in the shade of a wild cherry tree, and watched the sun shifting through the branches as it rose over the hill called Pari Tibba (Fairy Hill) and slid down the steep slope into the valley. The air was very still and already the birds were silent. The only sound came from the water running over the stony bed of the stream. I had lain there ten, perhaps fifteen, minutes when I began to feel that someone was watching me.

Someone in the trees, in the shadows, still and watchful. Nothing moved; not a stone shifted, not a twig broke, but someone was watching me. I felt terribly exposed—not to danger, but to the scrutiny of unknown eyes. So I left the rock and, finding a path through the trees, began climbing the hill again.

It was warm work. The sun was up, and there was no breeze. I was perspiring profusely by the time I got to the top of the hill. There was no sign of my unseen watcher. Two lean cows grazed on the short grass; the tinkling of their bells was the only sound in the sultry summer air.

That song again! The same song, the same singer. I heard her from my window. And putting aside the book I was reading, I leant out of the window and started down through the trees. But the foliage was too heavy, and the singer too far away for me to be able to make her out. 'Should I go and look for her?' I wondered. Or is it better this way—heard but not seen? For having fallen in love with a song, must it follow that I will fall in love with the singer? No. But surely it is the voice, and not the song that has touched me... Presently the singing ended, and I turned away from the window.

◆

A girl was gathering bilberries on the hillside. She was fresh-faced, honey-coloured; her lips were stained with purple juice. She smiled at me. 'Are they good to eat?' I asked.

She opened her fist and thrust out her hand, which was full of berries, bruised and crushed. I took one and put it in my mouth. It had a sharp, sour taste. 'It is good,' I said. Finding that I could speak haltingly in her language, she came nearer, said, 'Take more then,' and filled my hand with bilberries. Her fingers touched mine. The sensation was almost

Binya Passes By

unique, for it had been nine or ten years since my hand had touched a girl's.

'Where do you live?' I asked. She pointed across the valley to where a small village straddled the slopes of a terraced hill.

'It's quite far,' I said. 'Do you always come so far from home?'

'I go further than this,' she said. 'The cows must find fresh grass. And there is wood to gather and grass to cut.' She showed me the sickle held by the cloth tied firmly about her waist. 'Sometimes I go to the top of Pari Tibba, sometimes to the valley beyond. Have you been there?'

'No. But I will go some day.'

'It is always windy on Pari Tibba.'

'Is it true that there are fairies there?'

She laughed. 'That is what people say. But those are people who have never been there. I do not see fairies on Pari Tibba. It is said that there are ghosts in the ruins on the hill. But I do not see any ghosts.'

'I have heard of the ghosts,' I said. 'Two lovers who ran away and took shelter in a ruined cottage. At night there was a storm, and they were killed by lightning. Is it true, this story?'

'It happened many years ago, before I was born. I have heard the story. But there are no ghosts on Pari Tibba.'

'How old are you?' I asked.

'Fifteen, sixteen, I do not know for sure.'

'Doesn't your mother know?'

'She is dead. And my grandmother has forgotten. And my brother, he is younger than me and he's forgotten his own age. Is it important to remember?'

'No, it is not important. Not here, anyway. Not in the hills. To a mountain, a hundred years are but as a day.'

'Are you very old?' she asked.

'I hope not. Do I look very old?'

'Only a hundred,' she said, and laughed, and the silver bangles on her wrists tinkled as she put her hand up to her laughing face.

'Why do you laugh?' I asked.

'Because you looked as though you believed me. How old are you?'

'Thirty-five, thirty-six, I do not remember.'

'Ah, it is better to forget!'

'That's true,' I said, 'but sometimes one has to fill in forms and things like that, and then one has to state one's age.'

'I have never filled a form. I have never seen one.'

'And I hope you never will. It is a piece of paper covered with useless information. It is all a part of human progress.'

'Progress?'

'Yes. Are you unhappy?'

'No.'

'Do you go hungry?'

'No.'

'Then you don't need progress. Wild bilberries are better.'

She went away without saying goodbye. The cows had strayed and she ran after them, calling them by name: 'Neelu, Neelu!' (Blue) and 'Bhuri!' (Old One). Her bare feet moved swiftly over the rocks and dry grass.

◆

Early May. The cicadas were singing in the forests, or rather, orchestrating, since they make the sound with their legs. The whistling thrushes pursued each other over the treetops, in acrobatic love-flights. Sometimes the langoors visited the oak trees to feed on the leaves. As I moved down the path to the stream, I heard the same singing, and coming suddenly upon the clearing near the water's edge, I saw the girl sitting on a rock, her feet in the rushing water—the same girl who had given me bilberries. Strangely enough, I had not guessed that she was the singer. Unseen voices conjure up fanciful images. I had imagined a woodland nymph, a graceful, delicate, beautiful, goddess-like creature, not a mischievous-eyed, round-faced, juice-stained, slightly ragged pixie. Her dhoti—a rough, homespun sari—faded and torn: an impractical garment, I thought, for running about on the hillside, but the village folk put their girls into dhotis before they are twelve. She'd compromised by hitching it up, and by strengthening the waist with a length of cloth bound tightly about her, but she'd have been more at ease in the long, flounced skirt worn in the further hills.

But I was not disillusioned. I had clearly taken a fancy to her cherubic, open countenance, and the sweetness of her voice added to her charms.

I watched her from the banks of the stream, and presently she looked up, grinned, and stuck her tongue out at me.

'That's a nice way to greet me,' I said. 'Have I offended you?'

'You surprised me. Why did you not call out?'

'Because I was listening to your singing. I did not wish to speak until you had finished.'

'It was only a song.'

'But you sang it sweetly.'

She smiled. 'Have you brought anything to eat?'

'No. Are you hungry?'

'At this time I get hungry. When you come to meet me

you must always bring something to eat.'

'But I didn't come to meet you. I didn't know you would be here.'

'You do not wish to meet me?'

'I didn't mean that. It is nice to meet you.'

'You will meet me if you keep coming into the forest. So always bring something to eat.'

'I will do so next time. Shall I pick you some berries?'

'You will have to go to the top of the hill again to find the Kingora bushes.'

'I don't mind. If you are hungry, I will bring some.'

'All right,' she said, and looked down at her feet, which were still in the water.

Like some knight-errant of old, I toiled up the hill again until I found the bilberry bushes, and stuffing my pockets with berries, I returned to the stream. But when I got there I found she'd slipped away. The cowbells tinkled on the far hill.

♦

Glow worms shone fitfully in the dark. The night was full of sounds—the *tonk-tonk* of a nightjar, the cry of a barking deer, the shuffling of porcupines, the soft flip-flop of moths beating against the windowpanes. On the hill across the valley, lights flickered in the small village—the dim lights of kerosene lamps swinging in the dark.

'What is your name?' I asked, when we met again on the path through the pine forest.

'Binya,' she said. 'What is yours?'

'I've no name.'

'All right, Mr No-name.'

'I mean, I haven't made a name for myself. We must make our own names, don't you think?'

'Binya is my name. I do not wish to have any other. Where are you going?'

'Nowhere.'

'No-name goes nowhere! Then you cannot come with me, because I am going home and my grandmother will set the village dogs on you if you follow me.' And laughing, she ran down the path to the stream; she knew I could not catch up with her.

◆

Her face streamed summer rain as she climbed the steep hill, calling the white cow home. She seemed very tiny on the windswept mountainside; a twist of hair lay flat against her forehead and her torn blue dhoti clung to her firm round thighs. I went to her with an umbrella to give her shelter. She stood with me beneath the umbrella and let me put my arm around her. Then she turned her face up to mine, wonderingly, and I kissed her quickly, softly on the lips. Her lips tasted of raindrops and mint. And then she left me there, so gallant in the blistering rain. She ran home laughing. But it was worth the drenching.

Another day I heard her calling to me—'No-name, Mister No-name!'—but I couldn't see her, and it was some time before I found her, halfway up a cherry tree, her feet pressed firmly against the bark, her dhoti tucked up between her thighs—fair, rounded thighs, and legs that were strong and vigorous.

'The cherries are not ripe,' I said.

'They are never ripe. But I like them green and sour. Will you come into the tree?'

'If I can still climb a tree,' I said.

'My grandmother is over sixty, and *she* can climb trees.'

'Well, I wouldn't mind being more adventurous at sixty. There's not so much to lose then.' I climbed into the tree without much difficulty, but I did not think the higher branches would take my weight, so I remained standing in the fork of the tree, my face on a level with Binya's breasts. I put my hand against her waist, and kissed her on the soft inside of her arm. She did not say anything. But she took me by the hand and helped me to climb a little higher, and I put my arm around her, as much to support myself as to be close to her.

◆

The full moon rides high, shining through the tall oak trees near the window. The night is full of sounds, crickets, the *tonk-tonk* of a nightjar, and floating across the valley from your village, the sound of drums beating, and people singing. It is a festival day, and there will be feasting in your home. Are you singing too, tonight? And are you thinking of me, as you sing, as you laugh, as you dance with your friends? I am sitting here alone, and so I have no one to think of but you.

Binya... I take your name again and again—as though by taking it, I can make you hear me, come to me, walking over the moonlit mountain...

There are spirits abroad tonight. They move silently in the trees; they hover about the window at which I sit; they take up with the wind and rush about the house. Spirits of the trees, spirits of the old house. An old lady died here last year. She'd lived in the house for over thirty years; something of her personality surely dwells here still. When I look into the tall, old mirror which was hers, I sometimes catch a glimpse of her pale face and long, golden hair. She likes me, I think, and the house is kind to me. Would she be jealous of you, Binya?

The music and singing grows louder. I can imagine your face glowing in the firelight. Your eyes shine with laughter. You have all those people near you and I have only the stars, and the nightjar, and the ghost in the mirror.

◆

I woke early, while the dew was still fresh on the grass, and walked down the hill to the stream, and then up to a little knoll where a pine tree grew in solitary splendour, the wind going *hoo-hoo* in its slender branches. This was my favourite place, my place of power, where I came to renew myself from time to time. I lay on the grass, dreaming. The sky in its blueness swung round above me. An eagle soared in the distance. I heard her voice down among the trees, or I thought I heard it. But when I went to look, I could not find her.

I'd always prided myself on my rationality, had taught myself to be wary of emotional states, like 'falling in love', which turned out to be ephemeral and illusory. And although I told myself again and again that the attraction was purely physical, on my part as well as hers, I had to admit to myself that my feelings towards Binya differed from the feelings I'd had for others, and that while sex had often been for me a celebration, it had, like any other feast, resulted in satiety, a need for change, a desire to forget...

Binya represented something else—something wild, dreamlike, fairy-like. She moved close to the spirit-haunted rocks, the old trees, the young grass; she had absorbed something from them—a primeval innocence, an unconcern with the passing of time and events, an affinity with the forest and the mountains—this made her special and magical.

And so, when three, four, five days went by, and I did not find her on the hillside, I went through all the pangs of frustrated love: had she forgotten me and gone elsewhere? Had we been seen together, and was she being kept at home? Was she ill? Or, had she been spirited away?

I could hardly go and ask for her. I would probably be driven from the village. It straddled the opposite hill, a cluster of slate-roof houses, a pattern of little terraced fields. I could see figures in the fields, but they were too far away, too tiny for me to be able to recognize anyone. She had gone to her mother's village a hundred miles away, or so a small boy told me.

And so I brooded, walked disconsolately through the oak forest hardly listening to the birds—the sweet-throated whistling thrush, the shrill barbet, the mellow-voiced doves. Happiness had always made me more responsive to nature. Feeling miserable, my thoughts turned inward. I brooded upon the trickery of time and circumstance; I felt the years were passing by, *had* passed by, like waves on a receding tide, leaving me washed up like a bit of flotsam on a lonely beach. But at the same time, the whistling thrush seemed to mock at me, calling tantalizingly from the shadows of the ravine, 'It isn't time that's passing by, it is you and I, it is you and I…'

Then I forced myself to snap out of my melancholy. I kept away from the hillside and the forest. I did not look towards the village. I buried myself in my work, tried to think objectively, and wrote an article on 'The inscriptions on the iron pillar at Kalsi'—very learned, very dry, very sensible.

Binya Passes By

But at night I was assailed by the thoughts of Binya. I could not sleep. I switched on the light, and there she was, smiling at me from the looking glass, replacing the image of the old lady who had watched over me for so long.

THE STORY OF MADHU

I met little Madhu several years ago, when I lived alone in an obscure town near the Himalayan foothills. I was in my late twenties then, and my outlook on life was still quite romantic; the cynicism that was to come with the thirties had not yet set in.

I preferred the solitude of the small district town to the kind of social life I might have found in the cities, and in my books, my writing and the surrounding hills, there was enough for my pleasure and occupation.

On summer mornings I would often sit beneath an old mango tree, with a notebook or a sketch pad on my knees. The house which I had rented (for a very nominal sum) stood on the outskirts of the town, and a large tank and a few poor houses could be seen from the garden wall. A narrow public pathway passed under the low wall.

One morning, while I sat beneath the mango tree, I saw a young girl of about nine, wearing torn clothes, darting about on the pathway and along the high banks of the tank.

Sometimes she stopped to look at me, and, when I showed that I noticed her, she felt encouraged and gave me a shy, fleeting

The Story of Madhu

smile. The next day I discovered her leaning over the garden wall, following my actions as I paced up and down on the grass.

In a few days an acquaintance had been formed. I began to take the girl's presence for granted, and even to look for her, and she, in turn, would linger about on the pathway until she saw me come out of the house.

One day, as she passed the gate, I called her to me.

'What is your name?' I asked. 'And where do you live?'

'Madhu,' she said, brushing back her long untidy black hair and smiling at me from large black eyes. She pointed across the road: 'I live with my grandmother.'

'Is she very old?' I asked.

Madhu nodded confidingly and whispered: 'A hundred years...'

'We will never be that old,' I said. She was very slight and frail, like a flower growing in a rock, vulnerable to wind and rain.

I discovered later that the old lady was not her grandmother but a childless woman who had found the baby girl on the banks of the tank. Madhu's real parentage was unknown, but the wizened old woman had, out of compassion, brought up the child as her own.

My gate once entered, Madhu included the garden in her circle of activities. She was there every morning, chasing butterflies, stalking squirrels and myna, her voice brimming with laughter, her slight figure flitting about between the trees.

Sometimes, but not often, I gave her a toy or a new dress, and one day she put aside her shyness and brought me a present of a nosegay, made up of marigolds and wild blue-cotton flowers.

'For you,' she said, and put the flowers in my lap.

'They are very beautiful,' I said, picking out the brightest marigold and putting it in her hair. 'But they are not as beautiful as you.'

More than a year passed before I began to take more than a mildly patronizing interest in Madhu.

It occurred to me after some time that she should be taught to read and write, and I asked a local teacher to give her lessons in the garden for an hour every day. She clapped her hands with pleasure at the prospect of what was to be for her a fascinating new game.

In a few weeks Madhu was surprising us with her capacity for absorbing knowledge. She always came to me to repeat the lessons of the day, and pestered me with questions on a variety of subjects. How big was the world? And were the stars really like our world? Or were they the sons and daughters of the sun and the moon?

My interest in Madhu deepened, and my life, so empty till then, became imbued with a new purpose. As she sat on the grass beside me, reading aloud or listening to me with a look of complete trust and belief, all the love that had been lying dormant in me during my years of self-exile surfaced in a sudden surge of tenderness.

Three years glided away imperceptibly, and at the age of thirteen Madhu was on the verge of blossoming into a woman. I began to feel a certain responsibility towards her.

It was dangerous, I knew, to allow a child so pretty to live almost alone and unprotected, and to run unrestrained about the grounds. And in a censorious society she would be made to suffer if she spent too much time in my company.

She could see no need for any separation but I decided to send her to a mission school in the next district, where I could

The Story of Madhu

visit her from time to time.

'But why?' said Madhu. 'I can learn more from you, and from the teacher who comes. I am so happy here.'

'You will meet other girls and make many friends,' I told her. 'I will come to see you. And, when you come home, we will be even happier. It is good that you should go.'

It was the middle of June, a hot and oppressive month in the Siwaliks. Madhu had expressed her readiness to go to school, and when, one evening, I did not see her as usual in the garden, I thought nothing of it, but the next day I was informed that she had fever and could not leave the house.

Illness was something Madhu had not known before, and for this reason I felt afraid. I hurried down the path which led to the old woman's cottage. It seemed strange that I had never once entered it during my long friendship with Madhu.

It was a humble mud hut, the ceiling just high enough to enable me to stand upright, the room dark but clean. Madhu was lying on a string cot, exhausted by fever, her eyes closed, her long hair unkempt, one small hand hanging over the side.

It struck me then how little, during all this time, I had thought of her physical comforts. There was no chair; I knelt down, and took her hand in mine. I knew, from the fierce heat of her body, that she was seriously ill.

She recognized my touch, and a smile passed across her face before she opened her eyes. She held on to my hand, then laid it across her cheek.

I looked round the little room in which she had grown up. It had scarcely an article of furniture apart from two string cots, on one of which the old woman sat and watched us, her white, wizened head nodding like a puppet's.

In a corner lay Madhu's little treasures. I recognized among them the presents which during the past four years I had given her. She had kept everything. On her dark arm she still wore a small piece of ribbon which I had playfully tied there about a year ago. She had given her heart, even before she was conscious of possessing one, to a stranger unworthy of the gift. As the evening drew on, a gust of wind blew open the door of the dark room, and a gleam of sunshine streamed in, lighting up a portion of the wall. It was the time when every evening she would join me under the mango tree. She had been quiet for almost an hour, and now a slight pressure of her hand drew my eyes back to her face.

'What will we do now?' she said. 'When will you send me to school?'

'Not for a long time. First you must get well and strong. That is all that matters.'

She didn't seem to hear me. I think she knew she was dying, but she did not resent it happening.

'Who will read to you under the tree?' she went on. 'Who will look after you?' she asked, with the solicitude of a grown woman.

'You will, Madhu. You are grown up now. There will be no one else to look after me.'

The old woman was standing at my shoulder. A hundred years—and little Madhu was slipping away. The woman took Madhu's hand from mine, and laid it gently down. I sat by the cot a little longer, and then I rose to go, all the loneliness in the world pressing upon my heart.

WHO KISSED ME IN THE DARK?

This chapter, or story, could not have been written but for a phone call I received last week. I'll come to the caller later. Suffice to say that it triggered memories of a hilarious fortnight in the autumn of that year (can't remember which one) when India and Pakistan went to war with each other. It did not last long, but there was plenty of excitement in our small town, set off by a rumour that enemy parachutists were landing in force in the ravine below Pari Tibba.

The road to this ravine led past my dwelling, and one afternoon I was amazed to see the town's constabulary, followed by hundreds of concerned citizens (armed mostly with hockey sticks) taking the trail down to the little stream where I usually went bird-watching. The parachutes turned out to be bedsheets from a nearby school, spread out to dry by the dhobis who lived on the opposite hill. After days of incessant rain, the sun had come out, and the dhobis had finally got a chance to dry the school bedsheets on the verdant hillside. From afar they did look a bit like open parachutes. In times of crisis, it's wonderful what the imagination will do.

There were also black-outs. It's hard for a hill station to black itself out, but we did our best. Two or three respectable people were arrested for using their torches to find their way home in the dark. And of course, nothing could be done about the lights on the next mountain, as the people there did not even know there was a war on. They did not have radio or television or even electricity. They used kerosene lamps or lit bonfires!

We had a smart young set in Mussoorie in those days, mostly college students who had also been to convent schools and some of them decided it would be a good idea to put on a show—or old-fashioned theatrical extravaganza—to raise funds for the war effort. And they thought it would be a good idea to rope me in, as I was the only writer living in Mussoorie in those innocent times. I was thirty-one and I had never been a college student but they felt I was the right person to direct a one-act play in English. This was to be the centrepiece of the show.

I forget the name of the play. It was one of those drawing-room situation comedies popular from the 1920s, inspired by such successes as *Charley' Aunt* and *Tons of Money*. Anyway, we went into morning rehearsals at Hakman's, one of the older hotels, where there was a proper stage and a hall large enough to seat at least two hundred spectators.

The participants were full of enthusiasm, and rehearsals went along quite smoothly. They were an engaging bunch of young people—Guttoo, the intellectual among them; Ravi, a schoolteacher; Gita, a tiny ball of fire; Neena, a heavy-footed Bharatnatyam exponent; Nellie, daughter of a nurse; Chameli, who was in charge of make-up (she worked at a local beauty saloon); Rajiv, who served in the bar and was also our prompter; and a host of others, some of whom would sing and dance before and after our one-act play.

Who Kissed Me in the Dark?

The performance was well attended, Ravi having rounded up a number of students from the local schools, and the lights were working, although we had to cover all doors, windows and exits with blankets to maintain the regulatory black-out. But the stage was old and rickety and things began to go wrong during Neena's dance number when, after a dazzling pirouette, she began stamping her feet and promptly went through the floorboards. Well, to be precise, her lower half went through, while the rest of her remained above board and visible to the audience.

The schoolboys cheered, the curtain came down and we rescued Neena, who had to be sent to the civil hospital with a sprained ankle, Mussoorie's only civilian war casualty.

There was a hold-up, but before the audience could get too restless the curtain went up on our play, a tea-party scene, which opened with Guttoo pouring tea for everyone. Unfortunately, our stage manager had forgotten to put any tea in the pot and poor Guttoo looked terribly put out as he went from cup to cup, pouring invisible tea. 'Damn. What happened to the tea?' muttered Guttoo, a line, which was not in the script. 'Never mind,' said Gita, playing opposite him and keeping her cool. 'I prefer my milk without tea,' and proceeded to pour herself a cup of milk.

After this, everyone began to fluff their lines and our prompter had a busy time. Unfortunately, he'd helped himself to a couple of rums at the bar, so that, whenever one of the actors faltered, he'd call out the correct words in a stentorian voice which could be heard all over the hall. Soon there was more prompting than acting and the audience began joining in with dialogue of their own.

We Must Love Someone

Finally, to my great relief, the curtain came down—to thunderous applause. It went up again, and the cast stepped forward to take a bow. Our prompter, who was also the curtain-puller, released the ropes prematurely and the curtain came down with a rush, one of the sandbags hitting poor Guttoo on the head. He has never fully recovered from the blow.

The lights, which had been behaving all evening, now failed us, and we had a real black-out. In the midst of this confusion, someone—it must have been a girl, judging from the overpowering scent of jasmine that clung to her—put her arms around me and kissed me.

When the light came on again, she had vanished.

Who had kissed me in the dark?

As no one came forward to admit to the deed, I could only make wild guesses. But it had been a very sweet kiss, and I would have been only too happy to return it had I known its ownership. I could hardly go up to each of the girls and kiss them in the hope of reciprocation. After all, it might even have been someone from the audience.

Anyway, our concert did raise a few hundred rupees for the war effort. By the time we sent the money to the right authorities, the war was over. Hopefully they saw to it that the money was put to good use.

We went our various ways and although the kiss lingered in my mind, it gradually became a distant, fading memory and as the years passed it went out of my head altogether. Until the other day, almost forty years later...

'Phone for you,' announced Gautam, my seven-year-old secretary.

'Boy or girl? Man or woman?'

'Don't know. Deep voice like my teacher but it says you know her.'

'Ask her name.'

Gautam asked.

'She's Nellie, and she's speaking from Bareilly.'

'Nellie from Bareilly?' I was intrigued. I took the phone. 'Hello,' I said. 'I'm Bonda from Golconda.'

'Then you must be wealthy now.' Her voice was certainly husky. 'But don't you remember me? Nellie? I acted in that play of yours, up in Mussoorie a long time ago.'

'Of course, I remember now,' I was remembering. 'You had a small part, the maidservant I think. You were very pretty. You had dark, sultry eyes. But what made you ring me after all these years?'

'Well, I was thinking of you. I've often thought about you. You were much older than me, but I liked you. After that show, when the lights went out, I came up to you and kissed you. And then I ran away.'

'So it was you! I've often wondered. But why did you run away? I would have returned the kiss. More than once.'

'I was very nervous. I thought you'd be angry.'

'Well, I suppose it's too late now. You must be happily married with lots of children.'

'Husband left me. Children grew up, went away.'

'It must be lonely for you.'

'I have lots of dogs.'

'How many?'

'About thirty.'

'Thirty dogs! Do you run a kennel club?'

'No, they are all strays. I run a dog shelter.'

'Well, that's very good of you. Very humane.'

'You must come and see it sometime. Come to Bareilly. Stay with me. You like dogs, don't you?'

'Er—yes, of course. Man's best friend, the dog. But thirty is a lot of dogs to have about the house.'

'I have lots of space.'

'I'm sure... Well, Nellie, if ever I'm in Bareilly, I'll come to see you. And I'm glad you phoned and cleared up the mystery. It was a lovely kiss and I'll always remember it.'

We said our goodbyes and I promised to visit her some day. A trip to Bareilly to return a kiss might seem a bit far-fetched, but I've done sillier things in my life. It's those dogs that worry me. I can imagine them snapping at my heels as I attempt to approach their mistress. Dogs can be very possessive.

'Who was that on the phone?' asked Gautam, breaking in on my reverie.

'Just an old friend!'

'Dada's old girlfriend. Are you going to see her?'

'I'll think about it.'

And I'm still thinking about it and about those dogs. But bliss it was to be in Mussoorie forty years ago, when Nellie had kissed me in the dark.

Some memories are best left untouched.

THE GIRL ON THE TRAIN

I had the train compartment to myself up to Rohana, then a girl got in. The couple who saw her off were probably her parents; they seemed very anxious about her comfort, and the woman gave the girl detailed instructions as to where to keep her things, when not to lean out of windows, and how to avoid speaking to strangers.

They called their goodbyes and the train pulled out of the station. As I was going blind at the time, my eyes sensitive only to light and darkness, I was unable to tell what the girl looked like, but I knew she wore slippers from the way they slapped against her heels.

It would take me some time to discover something about her looks, and perhaps I never would. But I liked the sound of her voice, and even the sound of her slippers.

'Are you going all the way to Dehra?' I asked.

I must have been sitting in a dark corner, because my voice startled her. She gave a little exclamation and said, 'I didn't know anyone else was here.'

Well, it often happens that people with good eyesight fail to see what is right in front of them. They have too much to take in, I suppose. Whereas people who cannot see (or see very little) have to take in only the essentials, whatever registers most tellingly on their remaining senses.

'I didn't see you either,' I said. 'But I heard you come in.'

I wondered if I would be able to prevent her from discovering that I was blind. Provided I keep to my seat, I thought, it shouldn't be too difficult.

The girl said, 'I'm getting off at Saharanpur. My aunt is meeting me there.'

'Then I had better not get too familiar,' I replied. 'Aunts are usually formidable creatures.'

'Where are you going?' she asked.

'To Dehra, and then to Mussoorie.'

'Oh, how lucky you are. I wish I were going to Mussoorie. I love the hills. Especially in October.'

'Yes, this is the best time,' I said, calling on my memories. 'The hills are covered with wild dahlias, the sun is delicious, and at night you can sit in front of a logfire and drink a little brandy. Most of the tourists have gone, and the roads are quiet and almost deserted. Yes, October is the best time.'

She was silent. I wondered if my words had touched her, or whether she thought me a romantic fool. Then I made a mistake.

'What is it like outside?' I asked.

She seemed to find nothing strange in the question. Had she noticed already that I could not see? But her next question removed my doubts.

'Why don't you look out of the window?' she asked.

I moved easily along the berth and felt for the window ledge. The window was open, and I faced it, making a pretence of studying the landscape. I heard the panting of the engine,

The Girl on the Train

the rumble of the wheels, and, in my mind's eye, I could see telegraph posts flashing by.

'Have you noticed,' I ventured, 'that the trees seem to be moving while we seem to be standing still?'

'That always happens,' she said. 'Do you see any animals?'

'No,' I answered quite confidently. I knew that there were hardly any animals left in the forests near Dehra.

I turned from the window and faced the girl, and for a while we sat in silence.

'You have an interesting face,' I remarked. I was becoming quite daring, but it was a safe remark. Few girls can resist flattery. She laughed pleasantly—a clear ringing laugh.

'It's nice to be told I have an interesting face. I'm tired of people telling me I have a pretty face.'

Oh, so you do have a pretty face, thought I, and aloud I said, 'Well, an interesting face can also be pretty.'

'You are a very gallant young man,' she said 'but why are you so serious?'

I thought, then, I would try to laugh for her, but the thought of laughter only made me feel troubled and lonely.

'We'll soon be at your station,' I said.

'Thank goodness it's a short journey. I can't bear to sit in a train for more than two or three hours.'

Yet I was prepared to sit there for almost any length of time, just to listen to her talking. Her voice had the sparkle of a mountain stream. As soon as she left the train, she would forget our brief encounter, but it would stay with me for the rest of the journey, and for some time after.

The engine's whistle shrieked, the carriage wheels changed their sound and rhythm, the girl got up and began to collect her things. I wondered if she wore her hair in a bun, or if it was plaited; perhaps it was hanging loose over her shoulders, or was it cut very short?

The train drew slowly into the station. Outside, there was the shouting of porters and vendors and a high-pitched female voice near the carriage door—that voice must have belonged to the girl's aunt.

'Goodbye,' the girl said.

She was standing very close to me, so close that the perfume from her hair was tantalizing. I wanted to raise my hand and touch her hair, but she moved away. Only the scent of perfume still lingered where she had stood.

There was some confusion in the doorway. A man, getting into the compartment, stammered an apology. Then the door banged, and the world was shut out again. I returned to my berth. The guard blew his whistle and we moved off. Once again, I had a game to play and a new fellow traveller.

The train gathered speed, the wheels took up their song, the carriage groaned and shook. I found the window and sat in front of it, staring into the daylight that was darkness for me.

So many things were happening outside the window: it could be a fascinating game, guessing what went on out there.

The man who had entered the compartment broke into my reverie.

'You must be disappointed,' he said. 'I'm not nearly as attractive a travelling companion as the one who just left.'

'She was an interesting girl,' I said. 'Can you tell me—did she keep her hair long or short?'

'I don't remember,' he said, sounding puzzled. 'It was her eyes I noticed, not her hair. She had beautiful eyes—but they were of no use to her. She was completely blind. Didn't you notice?'

HIS NEIGHBOUR'S WIFE

No (said Arun, as we waited for dinner to be prepared), I did not fall in love with my neighbour's wife. It is not that kind of story.

Mind you, Leela was a most attractive woman. She was not beautiful or pretty but she was handsome. Hers was the firm, athletic body of a sixteen-year-old boy, free of any surplus flesh. She bathed morning and evening, oiling herself well, so that her skin glowed a golden-brown in the winter sunshine. Her lips were often coloured with paan-juice, but her teeth were perfect.

I was her junior by about five years, and she called me her 'younger brother'. Her husband, who was forty to her thirty-two, was an official in the Customs and Excise Department: an extrovert, a hard-drinking, backslapping man, who spent a great deal of time on tour. Leela knew that he was not always faithful to her during these frequent absences but she found solace in her own loyalty and in the well-being of her one child, a boy called Chandu.

I did not care for the boy. He had been well spoilt, and took great delight in disturbing me whenever I was at work. He entered my rooms uninvited, knocked my books about, and, if guests were present, made insulting remarks about them to their faces.

Leela, during her lonely evenings, would often ask me to sit on her veranda and talk to her. The day's work done, she would relax with a hookah. Smoking a hookah was a habit she had brought with her from her village near Agra, and it was a habit she refused to give up. She liked to talk and, as I was a good listener, she soon grew fond of me. The fact that I was twenty-six years old and still a bachelor, never failed to astonish her.

It was not long before she took upon herself the responsibility for getting me married. I found it useless to protest. She did not believe me when I told her that I could not afford to marry, that I preferred a bachelor's life. A wife, she insisted, was an asset to any man. A wife reduced expenses. Where did I eat? At a hotel, of course. That must cost me at least sixty rupees a month, even on a vegetarian diet. But if I had a simple homely wife to do the cooking, we could both eat well for less than that.

Leela fingered my shirt, observing that a button was missing and that the collar was frayed. She remarked on my pale face and general look of debility and told me that I would fall victim to all kinds of diseases if I did not find someone to look after me. What I needed, she declared between puffs at the hookah, was a woman—a young, healthy, buxom woman, preferably from a village near Agra.

'If I could find someone like you,' I said slyly, 'I would not mind getting married.'

She appeared neither flattered nor offended by my remark. 'Don't marry an older woman,' she advised. 'Never take a wife who is more experienced in the ways of the world than you are. You just leave it to me, I'll find a suitable bride for you.'

To please Leela, I agreed to this arrangement, thinking she would not take it seriously. But, two days later, when she suggested that I accompany her to a certain distinguished home for orphan girls, I became alarmed. I refused to have anything to do with her project.

'Don't you have confidence in me?' she asked. 'You said you would like a girl who resembled me. I know one who looks just as I did ten years ago.'

'I like you as you are now,' I said. 'Not as you were ten years ago.'

'Of course. We shall arrange for you to see the girl first.'

'You don't understand,' I protested. 'It's not that I feel I have to be in love with someone before marrying her—I know you would choose a fine girl, and I would really prefer someone who is homely and simple to an M.A. with Honours in Psychology—it's just that I'm not ready for it. I want another year or two of freedom. I don't want to be chained down. To be frank, I don't want the responsibility.'

'A little responsibility will make a man of you,' said Leela; but she did not insist on my accompanying her to the orphanage, and the matter was allowed to rest for a few days.

I was beginning to hope that Leela had reconciled herself to allowing one man to remain single in a world full of husbands when, one morning, she accosted me on the veranda with an open newspaper, which she thrust in front of my nose.

'There!' she said triumphantly. 'What do you think of that? I did it to surprise you.'

She had certainly succeeded in surprising me. Her henna-stained forefinger rested on an advertisement in the matrimonial columns.

Bachelor journalist, age twenty-five, seeks attractive young wife well-versed in household duties. Caste, religion no bar. Dowry optional.

I must admit that Leela had made a good job of it. In a few days the replies began to come in, usually from the parents of the girls concerned. Each applicant wanted to know how much money I was earning. At the same time, they took the trouble to list their own connections and the high positions occupied by relatives. Some parents enclosed their daughters' photographs. They were very good photographs, though there was a certain amount of touching-up employed.

I studied the pictures with interest. Perhaps marriage wasn't such a bad proposition, after all. I selected the photographs of the three girls I most fancied and showed them to Leela.

To my surprise, she disapproved of all three. One of the girls she said, had a face like a hermaphrodite; another obviously suffered from tuberculosis; and the third was undoubtedly an adventuress. Leela decided that the whole idea of the advertisement had been a mistake. She was sorry she had inserted it; the only replies we were likely to get would be from fortune hunters. And I had no fortune.

So we destroyed the letters. I tried to keep some of the photographs, but Leela tore them up too.

And so, for some time, there were no more attempts at getting me married.

Leela and I met nearly every day, but we spoke of other things. Sometimes, in the evenings, she would make me sit on the charpoy opposite her, and then she would draw up her hookah and tell me stories about her village and her family. I was getting used to the boy, too, and even growing rather fond of him.

All this came to an end when Leela's husband went and got himself killed. He was shot by a bootlegger who had decided to get rid of the excise man rather than pay him an exorbitant sum of money. It meant that Leela had to give up her quarters and return to her village near Agra. She waited until the boy's school term had finished, and then she packed their things and bought two tickets, third-class to Agra.

Something, I could see, had been troubling her, and when I saw her off at the station I realized what it was. She was having a fit of conscience about my continued bachelorhood.

'In my village,' she said confidently, leaning out from the carriage window, 'there is a very comely young girl, a distant relative of mine, I shall speak to the parents.'

And then I said something which I had not considered before; which had never, until that moment, entered my head. And I was no less surprised than Leela when the words came tumbling out of my mouth: 'Why don't *you* marry me now?'

Arun didn't have time to finish his story because, just at this interesting stage, the dinner arrived.

But the dinner brought with it the end of his story.

It was served by his wife, a magnificent woman, strong and handsome, who could only have been Leela. And a few minutes later, Chandu, Arun's stepson, charged into the house, complaining that he was famished.

Arun introduced me to his wife, and we exchanged the usual formalities.

'But why hasn't your friend brought his family with him?' she asked.

'Family? Because he's still a bachelor!'

And then as he watched his wife's expression change from a look of mild indifference to one of deep concern, he hurriedly changed the subject.

CALYPSO CHRISTMAS

My first Christmas in London had been a lonely one. My small bed-sitting-room near Swiss Cottage had been cold and austere, and my landlady had disapproved of any sort of revelry. Moreover, I hadn't the money for the theatre or a good restaurant. That first English Christmas was spent sitting in front of a lukewarm gas-fire, eating beans on toast, and drinking cheap sherry. My one consolation was the row of Christmas cards on the mantelpiece—most of them from friends in India.

But in the following year I was making more money and living in a bigger, brighter, homelier room. The new landlady approved of my bringing friends—even girls—to the house, and had even made me a plum pudding so that I could entertain my guests. My friends in London included a number of Indian and Commonwealth students, and through them I met George, a friendly, sensitive person from Trinidad.

George was not a student. He was over thirty. Like thousands of other West Indians, he had come to England because he had been told that jobs were plentiful, that there was a free health scheme and national insurance, and that he could earn anything from ten to twenty pounds a week—far more than he could make in Trinidad or Jamaica. But, while it was true that jobs were to be had in England, it was also true that sections of local labour resented outsiders filling these posts. There were also those, belonging chiefly to the lower middle-classes, who were prone to various prejudices, and though these people were a minority, they were still capable of making themselves felt and heard.

In any case, London is a lonely place, especially for the stranger. And for the happy-go-lucky West Indian, accustomed to sunshine, colour and music, London must he quite baffling.

As though to match the grey-green fogs of winter, Londoners wore sombre colours, greys and browns. The West Indians couldn't understand this. Surely, they reasoned, during a grey season the colours worn should be vivid reds and greens—colours that would defy the curling fog and uncomfortable rain? But Londoners frowned on these gay splashes of colour: to them it all seemed an expression of some sort of barbarism. And then again Londoners had a horror of any sort of loud noise, and a blaring radio could (quite justifiably) bring in scores of protests from neighbouring houses. The West Indians, on the other hand, liked letting off steam; they liked holding parties in their rooms at which there was much singing and shouting. They had always believed that England was their mother country, and so, despite rain, fog, sleet and snow, they were determined to live as they had lived back home in Trinidad. And it is to their credit, and even to the credit of indigenous Londoners, that this is what they succeeded in doing.

George worked for the British Railways. He was a ticket-collector at one of the underground stations; he liked his work, and received about ten pounds a week for collecting tickets. A large, stout man, with huge hands and feet, he always had a gentle, kindly expression on his mobile face. Amongst other accomplishments he could play the piano, and as there was an old, rather dilapidated piano in my room, he would often come over in the evenings to run his fat, heavy fingers over the keys, playing tunes that ranged from hymns to jazz pieces. I thought he would he a nice person to spend Christmas with, so I asked him to come and share the pudding my landlady had made, and a bottle of sherry I had procured.

Little did I realize that an invitation to George would he interpreted as an invitation to all of George's friends and relations—in fact, anyone who had known him in Trinidad—but this was the way he looked at it, and at eight o' clock on Christmas Eve, while a chilly wind blew dead leaves down from Hampstead Heath, I saw a veritable army of West Indians marching down Belsize Avenue, with George in the lead.

Bewildered, I opened my door to them, and in streamed George, George's cousins, George's nephews and George's friends. They were all smiling and shaking hands with me, making complimentary remarks about my room ('Man, that's some piano!' 'Hey, look at that crazy picture!' 'This rocking chair gives me fever!') and took no time at all to feel and make themselves at home. Everyone had brought something along for the party. George had brought several bottles of beer. Eric, a flashy, coffee-coloured youth, had brought cigarettes and more beer. Marian, a buxom woman of thirty-five, who called me 'darling' as soon as we met, and kissed me on the cheeks saying she adored pink cheeks, had brought bacon and eggs. Her daughter Lucy, who was sixteen and in the full bloom of youth, had brought a gramophone, while the little nephews carried the records. Other friends and familiars had also brought beer, and one enterprising fellow produced a bottle of Jamaican rum.

Then everything began to happen at once.

Lucy put a record on the gramophone, and the strains of *Basin Street Blues* filled the room. At the same time George sat down at the piano to hammer out an accompaniment to the record: his huge hands crushed down on the keys as though he were chopping up chunks of meat. Marian had lit the gas-fire and was busy frying bacon and eggs. Eric was opening beer bottles. In the midst of the noise and confusion I heard a knock on the door—a very timid, hesitant sort of knock—and opening it, found my landlady standing on the threshold.

'Oh, Mr Bond, the neighbours—' she began, and glancing into the room was rendered speechless.

'It's only tonight,' I said. 'They'll all go home after an hour. Remember, it's Christmas!'

She nodded mutely and hurried away down the corridor, pursued by something called *Be-Bop-A-Lola*. I closed the door and drew all the curtains in an effort to stifle the noise, but everyone was stamping about on the floorboards, and I hoped fervently that the downstairs people had gone to the theatre. George had started playing calypso music, and Eric and Lucy were strutting and stomping in the middle of the room, while the two nephews were improvising on their own. Before I knew what was happening, Marian had taken me in her strong arms, and was teaching me to do the calypso. The song playing, I think, was 'Banana Boat Song'.

Instead of the party lasting an hour, it lasted three hours. We ate innumerable fried eggs and finished off all the beer. I took turns dancing with Marian, Lucy and the nephews. There was a peculiar expression they used when excited. 'Fire!' they shouted. I never knew what was supposed to be on fire, or what the exclamation implied, but I too shouted 'Fire!' and somehow it seemed a very sensible thing to shout.

Perhaps their hearts were on fire, I don't know, but for all their excitability and flashiness and brashness they were lovable and sincere friends, and today, when I look back on my two years in London, that Christmas party is the brightest, most vivid memory of all, and the faces of George and Marian, Lucy and Eric, are the faces I remember best.

At midnight someone turned out the light. I was dancing with Lucy at the time, and in the dark she threw her arms around me and kissed me full on the lips. It was the first time I had been kissed by a girl, and when I think about it, I am glad that it was Lucy who kissed me.

When they left, they went in a bunch, just as they had come. I stood at the gate and watched them saunter down the dark, empty street. The buses and tubes had stopped running at midnight, and George and his friends would have to walk all the way back to their rooms at Highgate and Golders Green.

After they had gone, the street was suddenly empty and silent, and my own footsteps were the only sounds I could hear. The cold came clutching at me, and I turned up my collar. I looked up at the windows of my house, and at the windows of all the other houses in the street. They were all in darkness. It seemed to me that we were the only ones who had really celebrated Christmas.

THE GARLANDS ON HIS BROW

Fame has but a fleeting hold
On the reins in our fast-paced society;
So many of yesterday's heroes crumble.

Shortly after my return from England, I was walking down the main road of my old hometown of Dehra, gazing at the shops and passers-by to see what changes, if any, had taken place during my absence. I had been away three years. Still a boy when I went abroad, I was twenty-one when I returned with some mediocre qualifications to flaunt in the faces of my envious friends. (I did not tell them of the loneliness of those years in exile; it would not have impressed them.) I was nearing the clock tower when I met a beggar coming from the opposite direction. In one respect, Dehra had not changed. The beggars were as numerous as ever, though I must admit they looked healthier.

This beggar had a straggling beard, a hunch, a cavernous chest and unsteady legs on which a number of purple sores were festering. His shoulders looked as though they had once been powerful, and his hands thrusting a begging bowl at me, were still strong.

The Garlands on His Brow

He did not seem sufficiently decrepit to deserve my charity, and I was turning away when I thought I discerned a gleam of recognition in his eyes. There was something slightly familiar about the man; perhaps he was a beggar who remembered me from earlier years. He was even attempting a smile, showing me a few broken yellow fangs, and to get away from him, I produced a coin, dropped it in his bowl and hurried away.

I had gone about a hundred yards when, with a rush of memory, I knew the identity of the beggar. He was the hero of my childhood, Hassan, the most magnificent wrestler in the entire district.

I turned and retraced my steps, half hoping I wouldn't be able to catch up with the man and he had indeed got lost in the bazaar crowd. Well, I would doubtless be confronted by him again in a day or two. Leaving the road, I went into the municipal gardens and, stretching myself out on the fresh green February grass, allowed my memory to journey back to the days when I was a boy of ten, full of health and optimism, when my wonder at the great game of living had yet to give way to disillusionment at its shabbiness.

On those precious days when I played truant from school—and I would have learnt more had I played truant more often—I would sometimes make my way to the akhara at the corner of the gardens to watch the wrestling pit. My chin cupped in my hands, I would lean against a railing and gaze in awe at the rippling muscles, applauding with the other watchers whenever one of the wrestlers made a particularly clever move or pinned an opponent down on his back.

Amongst these wrestlers the most impressive and engaging young man was Hassan, the son of a kitemaker. He had a magnificent build, with great wide shoulders and powerful legs, and what he lacked in skill he made up for in sheer animal strength and vigour. The idol of all small boys, he was followed about by large numbers of us, and I was a particular favourite of his. He would offer to lift me on to his shoulders and carry me across the akhara to introduce me to his friends and fellow wrestlers.

From being Dehra's champion, Hassan soon became the outstanding representative of his art in the entire district. His technique improved, he began using his brain in addition to his brawn, and it was said by everyone that he had the makings of a national champion.

It was during a large fair towards the end of the rains that destiny took a hand in the shaping of his life. The Rani of — was visiting the fair, and she stopped to watch the wrestling bouts. When she saw Hassan stripped and in the ring, she began to take more than a casual interest in him. It has been said that she was a woman of a passionate and amoral nature, who could not be satisfied by her weak and ailing husband. She was struck by Hassan's perfect manhood, and through an official offered him the post of her personal bodyguard.

The Rani was rich and, in spite of having passed her fortieth summer, was a warm and attractive woman. Hassan did not find it difficult to make love according to the bidding, and on the whole he was happy in her service. True, he did not wrestle as often as in the past, but when he did enter a competition, his reputation and his physique combined to overawe his opponents, and they did not put up much resistance. One or two well-known wrestlers were invited to the district. The Rani paid them liberally, and they permitted Hassan to throw them out of the ring. Life in the Rani's house was comfortable and easy,

The Garlands on His Brow

and Hassan, a simple man, felt himself secure. And it is to the credit of the Rani (and also of Hassan) that she did not tire of him as quickly as she had of others.

But ranis, like washerwomen, are mortal, and when a long-standing and neglected disease at last took its toll, robbing her at once of all her beauty, she no longer struggled against it, but allowed it to poison and consume her once magnificent body. It would be wrong to say that Hassan was heartbroken when she died. He was not a deeply emotional or sensitive person. Though he could attract the sympathy of others, he had difficulty in producing any of his own. His was of kind but not compassionate nature.

He had served the Rani well, and what he was most aware of now was that he was without a job and without any money. The Raja had his own personal amusements and did not want a wrestler who was beginning to sag a little about the waist.

Times had changed. Hassan's father was dead, and there was no longer a living to be had from making kites; so Hassan returned to doing what he had always done: wrestling. But there was no money to be made at the akhara. It was only in the professional arena that a decent living could be made. And so, when a travelling circus of professionals—a Negro, a Russian, a Cockney-Chinese and a giant Sikh—came to town and offered a hundred rupees and a contract to the challenger who could stay five minutes in the ring with any one of them, Hassan took up the challenge.

He was pitted against the Russian, a bear of a man, who wore a black mask across his eyes, and in two minutes Hassan's Dehra supporters saw their hero slung about the ring, kicked in the head and groin, and finally flung unceremoniously through the ropes.

After this humiliation, Hassan did not venture into competitive bouts again. I saw him sometimes at the akhara, where he made a few rupees giving lessons to children. He had a paunch, and folds were beginning to accumulate beneath his chin. I was no longer a small boy, but he always had a smile and a hearty backslap reserved for me.

I remember seeing him a few days before I went abroad. He was moving heavily about the akhara; he had lost the lightning swiftness that had once made him invincible. Yes, I told myself.

The garlands wither on your brow;
They boast no more your mighty deeds…

That had been over three years ago. And for Hassan to have been reduced to begging was indeed a sad reflection of both the passing of time and the changing times. Fifty years ago, a popular local wrestler would never have been allowed to fall into a state of poverty and neglect. He would have been fed by his old friends, and stories would have been told of his legendary prowess. He would not have been forgotten. But those were more leisurely times, when the individual had his place in society, when a man was praised for his past achievement, and his failures were tolerated and forgiven. But life had since become fast and cruel and unreflective, and people were too busy counting their gains to bother about the idols of their youth.

It was a few days after my last encounter with Hassan that I found a small crowd gathered at the side of the road, not far from the clock tower. They were staring impassively at something in the drain, at the same time keeping a discreet distance. Joining the group, I saw that the object of their disinterested curiosity was a corpse, its head hidden under a culvert, legs protruding into the open drain. It looked as though the man had crawled into the drain to die, and had done so with his head in the culvert so the world would not witness his last unavailing struggle.

When the municipal workers came in their van, and lifted the body out of the gutter, a cloud of flies and bluebottles rose from the corpse with an angry buzz of protest. The face was muddy, but I recognized the beggar who was Hassan.

In a way, it was a consolation to know that he had been forgotten, that no one present could recognize the remains of the man who had once looked like a young god. I did not come forward to identify the body. Perhaps I saved Hassan from one final humiliation.

THE WOMAN ON PLATFORM NO. 8

It was MY second year at boarding school, and I was sitting on platform no. 8 at Ambala station, waiting for the northern-bound train. I think I was about twelve at the time. My parents considered me old enough to travel alone, and I had arrived by bus at Ambala early in the evening; now there was a wait till midnight before my train arrived. Most of the time I had been pacing up and down the platform, browsing through the bookstall, or feeding broken biscuits to stray dogs; trains came and went, the platform would be quiet for a while and then, when a train arrived, it would be an inferno of heaving, shouting, agitated human bodies. As the carriage doors opened, a tide of people would sweep down upon the nervous little ticket collector at the gate, and every time this happened I would be caught in the rush and swept outside the station. Now tired of this game and of ambling about the platform, I sat down on my suitcase and gazed dismally across the railway tracks.

Trolleys rolled past me, and I was conscious of the cries of the various vendors—the men who sold curds and lemon, the sweetmeat seller, the newspaper boy—but I had lost interest in all that was going on along the busy platform, and continued to

The Woman on Platform No. 8

stare across the railway tracks, feeling bored and a little lonely.

'Are you all alone, my son?' asked a soft voice close behind me.

I looked up and saw a woman standing near me. She was leaning over, and I saw a pale face and dark, kind eyes. She wore no jewels, and was dressed very simply in a white sari.

'Yes, I am going to school,' I said, and stood up respectfully. She seemed poor, but there was a dignity about her that commanded respect.

'I have been watching you for some time,' she said. 'Didn't your parents come to see you off?'

'I don't live here,' I said. 'I had to change trains. Anyway, I can travel alone.'

'I am sure you can,' she said, and I liked her for saying that, and I also liked her for the simplicity of her dress, and for her deep, soft voice and the serenity of her face.

'Tell me, what is your name?' she asked.

'Arun,' I said.

'And how long do you have to wait for your train?'

'About an hour, I think. It comes at twelve o'clock.'

'Then come with me and have something to eat.'

I was going to refuse, out of shyness and suspicion, but she took me by the hand, and then I felt it would be silly to pull my hand away. She told a coolie to look after my suitcase, and then she led me away down the platform. Her hand was gentle, and she held mine neither too firmly nor too lightly. I looked up at her again. She was not young. And she was not old. She must have been over thirty, but had she been fifty, I think she would have looked much the same.

She took me into the station dining room, ordered tea and samosas and jalebis, and at once I began to thaw and take a new interest in this kind woman. The strange encounter had little effect on my appetite. I was a hungry schoolboy, and I ate as much as I could in as polite a manner as possible. She took obvious pleasure in watching me eat, and I think it was the food that strengthened the bond between us and cemented our friendship, for under the influence of the tea and sweets I began to talk quite freely, and told her about my school, my friends, my likes and dislikes. She questioned me quietly from time to time, but preferred listening; she drew me out very well, and I had soon forgotten that we were strangers. But she did not ask me about my family or where I lived, and I did not ask her where she lived. I accepted her for what she had been to me—a quiet, kind and gentle woman who gave sweets to a lonely boy on a railway platform…

After about half an hour we left the dining room and began walking back along the platform. An engine was shunting up and down beside platform no. 8, and as it approached, a boy leapt off the platform and ran across the rails, taking a short cut to the next platform. He was at a safe distance from the engine, but as he leapt across the rails, the woman clutched my arm. Her fingers dug into my flesh, and I winced with pain. I caught her fingers and looked up at her, and I saw a spasm of pain and fear and sadness pass across her face. She watched the boy as he climbed the platform, and it was not until he had disappeared in the crowd that she relaxed her hold on my arm. She smiled at me reassuringly and took my hand again, but her fingers trembled against mine.

'He was all right,' I said, feeling that it was she who needed reassurance.

She smiled gratefully at me and pressed my hand. We walked

The Woman on Platform No. 8

together in silence until we reached the place where I had left my suitcase. One of my schoolfellows, Satish, a boy of about my age, had turned up with his mother.

'Hello, Arun!' he called. 'The train's coming in late, as usual. Did you know we have a new headmaster this year?'

We shook hands, and then he turned to his mother and said: 'This is Arun, Mother. He is one of my friends, and the best bowler in the class.'

'I am glad to know that,' said his mother, a large imposing woman who wore spectacles. She looked at the woman who held my hand and said: 'And I suppose you're Arun's mother?'

I opened my mouth to make some explanation, but before I could say anything, the woman replied: 'Yes, I am Arun's mother.'

I was unable to speak a word. I looked quickly up at the woman, but she did not appear to be at all embarrassed, and was smiling at Satish's mother.

Satish's mother said: 'It's such a nuisance having to wait for the train right in the middle of the night. But one can't let the child wait here alone. Anything can happen to a boy at a big station like this—there are so many suspicious characters hanging about. These days one has to be very careful of strangers.'

'Arun can travel alone, though,' said the woman beside me, and somehow I felt grateful to her for saying that. I had already forgiven her for lying, and besides, I had taken an instinctive dislike to Satish's mother.

'Well, be very careful, Arun,' said Satish's mother looking sternly at me through her spectacles. 'Be very careful when your mother is not with you. And never talk to strangers!'

I looked from Satish's mother to the woman who had given me tea and sweets, and back at Satish's mother.

'I like strangers,' I said.

Satish's mother definitely staggered a little, as obviously she was not used to being contradicted by small boys. 'There you are, you see! If you don't watch over them all the time, they'll walk straight into trouble. Always listen to what your mother tells you,' she said, wagging a fat little finger at me. 'And never, never talk to strangers.'

I glared resentfully at her, and moved closer to the woman who had befriended me. Satish was standing behind his mother, grinning at me, and delighting in my clash with his mother. Apparently he was on my side.

The station bell clanged, and the people who had till now been squatting resignedly on the platform began bustling about.

'Here it comes!' shouted Satish, as the engine whistle shrieked and the front lights played over the rails.

The train moved slowly into the station, the engine hissing and sending out waves of steam. As it came to a stop, Satish jumped on the footboard of a lighted compartment and shouted, 'Come on, Arun, this one's empty!' and I picked up my suitcase and made a dash for the open door.

We placed ourselves at the open windows, and the two women stood outside on the platform, talking up to us. Satish's mother did most of the talking.

'Now don't jump on and off moving trains, as you did just now,' she said. 'And don't stick your heads out of the windows, and don't eat any rubbish on the way.' She allowed me to share the benefit of her advice, as she probably didn't think my 'mother' a very capable person. She handed Satish a bag of fruit, a cricket bat and a big box of chocolates, and told him to share the food with me. Then she stood back from the window to watch how my 'mother' behaved.

I was smarting under the patronizing tone of Satish's mother, who obviously thought mine a very poor family, and I did not intend giving the other woman away. I let her take my hand in hers, but I could think of nothing to say. I was conscious of Satish's mother staring at us with hard, beady eyes, and I found myself hating her with a firm, unreasoning hate. The guard walked up the platform, blowing his whistle for the train to leave. I looked straight into the eyes of the woman who held my hand, and she smiled in a gentle, understanding way. I leaned out of the window then, and put my lips to her cheek and kissed her.

The carriage jolted forward, and she drew her hand away.

'Goodbye, Mother!' said Satish, as the train began to move slowly out of the station. Satish and his mother waved to each other.

'Goodbye,' I said to the other woman, 'Goodbye—Mother...' I didn't wave or shout, but sat still in front of the window, gazing at the woman on the platform. Satish's mother was talking to her, but she didn't appear to be listening; she was looking at me, as the train took me away. She stood there on the busy platform, a pale sweet woman in white, and I watched her until she was lost in the milling crowd.

MRS ROBERTS

Elsie Roberts had been quite a beauty in her twenties and thirties—one of those fair Anglo-Indians who passed for European until their accents gave them away. Elsie, it was said, did her best to remain fair, staying out of the sun as much as possible. In her later years, she was seldom seen during the day but by then she had lost her looks and taken to drink; she slept by day and lived by night.

In her heyday Elsie (nee MacGowan) was a dancing partner to Roberts, a good-looking French Jew who had made his way to India just before World War II broke out. They danced in Cabaret at the Imperial and Swiss in Delhi and at Hakman's in Mussoorie and Filetto's in Lahore. They made an elegant pair—they danced beautifully. Inevitably, they were compared to Fred Astaire and Ginger Rogers, the dancing sensation of the silver screen. They married and continued to partner each other until the war ended. Then, Roberts made a trip to France to claim and collect some compensation due to him as a war refugee. As he stood at the cashier's counter, waiting for the first instalment to be handed over to him, he collapsed and died of a heart attack. Chance gives and takes away, and sometimes

Mrs Roberts

gives again, but human life is equally unpredictable.

However, Elsie, as his widow, was entitled to the proceeds. She gave up her dancing career and took to breeding dogs. I first saw her when she came to see my mother in New Delhi, sometime in 1958. My mother was breeding Poms, and Elsie bought a small black Pom. She was still very attractive (Elsie, not the Pom) and was escorted by a gentleman who owned a small restaurant in Mussoorie.

'He's after the money,' said my mother later and she was right, as the gentleman in question wheedled a large sum of money out of her and then deserted her.

Elsie transferred her affections to her dogs. She rented a house outside Mussoorie and provided board and lodging to a large variety of canines. There was considerable inbreeding. Poms wed dachshunds, Samoyeds wed spaniels and Labradors wed German shepherds. The resultant mixture was undistinguished, to say the least. Elsie didn't care. She had become devoted to her dogs and had no desire to sell them, with or without pedigree. She fed them well and the local butcher proclaimed that she was his best customer.

Of course, strays and village dogs also found their way onto the premises. When there are free lunches to be had, dogs and humans are no different. Word soon gets around and everyone drops in for the wedding feast.

They were not a ferocious lot. Like their owner, they were wary of humans, quite paranoid about them. They'd bark furiously but scatter at the approach of anything on two legs.

When I came to live in Mussoorie in the mid-1960s, I thought I'd pay a casual visit to Mrs Roberts; my mother had asked me to look her up. She was then living near Barlowganj where she had a huge bungalow to herself, most of it occupied by some twenty to thirty dogs.

At first she refused to see me but when I told her who I was, she let me in. 'So you're Edie's son,' she said. 'How is your mother?'

'Not too well, I'm afraid.'

'Does she still have her Poms?'

'Several of them.' I refrained from adding that they were a bloody nuisance. Try sharing a Delhi flat with half a dozen snapping, yapping, highly strung, hysterical Poms—my least favourite breed!

Mrs Roberts showed me around. The house was filthy. She was equally unkempt—her dress soiled, hands and feet unwashed, hair all over the place. Only traces of her former beauty remained. She was in her late forties and fading fast.

But she was to live another twenty years.

The next time I saw her, about five years later, she was in considerable distress. Two or three of her dogs were suffering from mange and had to be put down. But the vet's injections hadn't worked properly (it was probably some spurious stuff) and the dogs died slowly and painfully. Mrs Roberts went further into her shell and moved with her companions to the top of the mountain, near Sister's Bazaar. Old-timers in that area still remember her.

She would emerge from her house once a month to collect her money from the local bank. The rest of the time she would remain locked up with her dogs, emerging only to receive the butcher or the milkman, who also brought her the local brew, a potent distillation made from mysterious ingredients. At the time we were going through a period of Prohibition (it was

Morarji's government), but Mrs Roberts and the local villagers had beaten the system.

I, too, had come to rely on the local milkman as a source of supply, 'English wines and spirits' having been taken off the market. Kachi-sharab, the special from Kotti, Kanda and other gaons, was the only alternative. My milkman used my hot-water bottle to bring me the stuff. Unfortunately, the hot-water bottle stank for weeks afterwards and could no longer be used for legitimate purposes. No matter. Those were desperate times.

Mrs Roberts had been on the stuff for years and was apparently none the worse for it. Prohibition came and went and politicians came and went and while frail creatures such as I returned to mere whisky and water; tougher souls, such as Elsie Roberts, continued with the local stuff, which was certainly more potent.

Two or three years passed and I had forgotten Mrs Roberts and her dog, when one morning the local missionary doctor, Dr Olsen, dropped in to tell me she had died in the night (of double pneumonia) and did I know if she had any relatives.

'None that I know of,' I had to say, 'just those dogs.'

She was given a pauper's burial in the little burial ground below Woodstock, where some of the school's Christian servants were laid to rest. No tombstones there. As a beautiful young dancer she'd been the toast of Mussoorie. That had been over forty years ago. Now, friendless, she had been swept away like a dead leaf.

And what of the dogs?

Bereft of their benefactor and bewildered by her absence, they ran wild. Some fled into the forest and perished. A few survived, along with the many street dogs that proliferate around the hill station.

We Must Love Someone

If you see a dog that looks especially weird (bits of terrier, spaniel, Pom and dachshund), you'll know it's descended from one of Mrs Roberts' pets. She did leave us a legacy of sorts.

FROM SMALL BEGINNINGS

And the last puff of the day-wind brought from the unseen villages the scent of damp wood-smoke, hot cakes, dripping undergrowth, and rotting pine-cones. That is the true smell of the Himalayas, and if once it creeps into the blood of a man, that man will at the last, forgetting all else, return to the hills to die.

—Rudyard Kipling

On the first clear September day, towards the end of the rains, I visited the pine knoll, my place of peace and power.

It was months since I'd last been there. Trips to the plains, a crisis in my affairs, involvements with other people and their troubles, and an entire monsoon had come between me and the grassy, pine-topped slope facing the Hill of Fairies (Pari Tibba to the locals). Now I tramped through late monsoon foliage—tall ferns, bushes festooned with flowering convolvulus—and crossed the stream by way of its little bridge of stones before climbing the steep hill to the pine slope.

When the trees saw me, they made as if to turn in my

direction. A puff of wind came across the valley from the distant snows. A long-tailed blue magpie took alarm and flew noisily out of an oak tree. The cicadas were suddenly silent. But the trees remembered me. They bowed gently in the breeze and beckoned me nearer, welcoming me home. Three pines, a straggling oak and a wild cherry. I went among them and acknowledged their welcome with a touch of my hand against their trunks—the cherry's smooth and polished; the pine's patterned and whorled; the oak's rough, gnarled, full of experience. He'd been there longest, and the wind had bent his upper branches and twisted a few, so that he looked shaggy and undistinguished. But like the philosopher who is careless about his dress and appearance, the oak has secrets, a hidden wisdom. He has learnt the art of survival!

While the oak and the pines are older than me and have been here many years, the cherry tree is exactly seven years old. 1 know, because I planted it.

One day I had this cherry seed in my hand, and on an impulse I thrust it into the soft earth, and then went away and forgot all about it. A few months later I found a tiny cherry tree in the long grass. I did not expect it to survive. But the following year it was two feet tall. And then some goats ate its leaves and a grass cutter's scythe injured the stem, and I was sure it would wither away. But it renewed itself, sprang up even faster, and within three years it was a healthy, growing tree, about five feet tall.

I left the hills for two years—forced by circumstances to make a living in Delhi—but this time I did not forget the cherry tree. I thought about it fairly often, sent telepathic messages of encouragement in its direction. And when, a couple of years ago,

I returned in the autumn, my heart did a somersault when I found my tree sprinkled with pale pink blossom. (The Himalayan cherry flowers in November.) And later, when the fruit was ripe, the tree was visited by finches, tits, bulbuls and other small birds, all come to feast on the sour, red cherries.

Last summer I spent a night on the pine knoll, sleeping on the grass beneath the cherry tree. I lay awake for hours, listening to the chatter of the stream and the occasional *tonk-tonk* of nightjars, and watching through the branches overhead, the stars turning in the sky. And I felt the power of the sky and the earth, and the power of a small cherry seed...

And so when the rains are over, this is where I come, that I might feel the peace and power of this place.

This is where I will write my stories. I can see everything from here—my cottage across the valley; behind and above me, the town and the bazaar, straddling the ridge; to the left, the high mountains and the twisting road to the source of the great river; below me, the little stream and the path to the village; ahead, the Hill of Fairies and the fields beyond; the wide valley below, and another range of hills and then the distant plains. I can even see Prem Singh in the garden, putting the mattresses out in the sun.

From here he is just a speck on the far hill, but I know it is Prem by the way he stands. A man may have a hundred disguises, but in the end it is his posture that gives him away. Like my grandfather, who was a master of disguise and successfully roamed the bazaars as fruit vendor or basket maker. But we could always recognize him because of his pronounced slouch.

Prem Singh doesn't slouch, but he has this habit of looking up at the sky (regardless of whether it's cloudy or clear), and at the moment he's looking at the sky.

Eight years with Prem. He was just a sixteen-year-old boy when I first saw him, and now he has a wife and child.

I had been in the cottage for just over a year... He stood on the landing outside the kitchen door. A tall boy, dark, with good teeth and brown, deep-set eyes, dressed smartly in white drill—his only change of clothes. Looking for a job. I liked the look of him, but—

'I already have someone working for me,' I said.

'Yes, sir. He is my uncle.'

In the hills, everyone is a brother or an uncle.

'You don't want me to dismiss your uncle?'

'No, sir. But he says you can find a job for me.'

'I'll try. I'll make inquiries. Have you just come from your village?'

'Yes. Yesterday I walked ten miles to Pauri. There I got a bus.'

'Sit down. Your uncle will make some tea.'

He sat down on the steps, removed his white keds, wriggled his toes. His feet were both long and broad, large feet but not ugly. He was unusually clean for a hill boy. And taller than most.

'Do you smoke?' I asked.

'No, sir.'

'It is true,' said his uncle. 'He does not smoke. All my nephews smoke but this one. He is a little peculiar, he does not smoke—neither beedi nor hookah.'

'Do you drink?'

'It makes me vomit.'

'Do you take bhang?'

'No, sahib.'

'You have no vices. It's unnatural.'

'He is unnatural, sahib,' said his uncle.

'Does he chase girls?'

'They chase him, sahib.'

'So he left the village and came looking for a job.' I looked at him. He grinned, then looked away and began rubbing his feet.

'Your name is...?'

'Prem Singh.'

'All right, Prem, I will try to do something for you.'

I did not see him for a couple of weeks. I forgot about finding him a job. But when I met him again, on the road to the bazaar, he told me that he had got a temporary job in the Survey, looking after the surveyor's tents.

'Next week we will be going to Rajasthan,' he said.

'It will be very hot. Have you been in the desert before?'

'No, sir.'

'It is not like the hills. And it is far from home.'

'I know. But I have no choice in the matter. I have to collect some money in order to get married.'

In his region there was a bride price, usually of two thousand rupees.

'Do you have to get married so soon?'

'I have only one brother and he is still very young. My mother is not well. She needs a daughter-in-law to help her in the fields and the house, and with the cows. We are a small family, so the work is greater.'

Every family has its few terraced fields, narrow and stony, usually perched on a hillside above a stream or river. They grow rice, barley, maize, potatoes—just enough to live on. Even if their produce is sufficient for marketing, the absence of roads makes it difficult to get the produce to the market towns. There is no money to be earned in the villages, and money is needed for clothes, soap, medicines, and for recovering the family jewellery from the moneylenders. So the young men leave their villages to find work, and to find work they must go to the plains. The lucky ones get into the army. Others enter domestic service or take jobs in garages, hotels, wayside tea shops, schools…

In Mussoorie the main attraction is the large number of schools which employ cooks and bearers. But the schools were full when Prem arrived. He'd been to the recruiting centre at Roorkee, hoping to get into the army, but they found a deformity in his right foot, the result of a bone broken when a landslip carried him away one dark monsoon night. He was lucky, he said, that it was only his foot and not his head that had been broken.

He came to the house to inform his uncle about the job and to say goodbye. I thought, another nice person I probably won't see again; another ship passing in the night, the friendly twinkle of its lights soon vanishing in the darkness. I said, 'Come again', held his smile with mine so that I could remember him better, and returned to my study and my typewriter. The typewriter is the repository of a writer's loneliness. It stares unsympathetically back at him every day, doing its best to be discouraging. Maybe I'll go back to the old-fashioned quill pen and marble inkstand; then I can feel like a real writer—Balzac or Dickens—scratching away into the endless reaches of the night… Of course, the days and nights are seemingly shorter than they need to be! They must be, otherwise why do we hurry so much and achieve so little, by the standards of the past…

Prem goes, disappears into the vast faceless cities of the plains, and a year slips by, or rather I do, and then here he is again, thinner and darker and still smiling and still looking for a job. I should have known that hillmen don't disappear altogether. The spirit-haunted rocks don't let their people wander too far, lest they lose them forever.

I was able to get him a job in the school. The headmaster's wife needed a cook. I wasn't sure if Prem could cook very well but I sent him along and they said they'd give him a trial. Three days later the headmaster's wife met me on the road and started gushing all over me. She was the type who gushed.

'We're so grateful to you! Thank you for sending me that lovely boy. He's so polite. And he cooks very well. A little too hot for my husband, but otherwise delicious—just delicious! He's a real treasure—a lovely boy.' And she gave me an arch look—the famous look which she used to captivate all the good-looking young prefects who became prefects, it was said, only if she approved of them.

I wasn't sure that she didn't want something more than a cook, and I only hoped that Prem would give every satisfaction.

He looked cheerful enough when he came to see me on his off day.

'How are you getting on?' I asked.

'Lovely,' he said, using his mistress's favourite expression.

'What do you mean—lovely? Do they like your work?'

'The memsahib likes it. She strokes me on the cheek whenever she enters the kitchen. The sahib says nothing. He takes medicine after every meal.'

'Did he always take medicine—or only now that you're doing the cooking?'

'I am not sure. I think he has always been sick.'

He was sleeping in the headmaster's veranda and getting sixty rupees a month. A cook in Delhi got a hundred and sixty.

And a cook in Paris or New York got ten times as much. I did not say as much to Prem. He might ask me to get him a job in New York. And that would be the last I saw of him! He, as a cook, might well get a job making curries off-Broadway; I, as a writer, wouldn't get to first base. And only my Uncle Ken knew the secret of how to make a living without actually doing any work. But then, of course, he had four sisters. And each of them was married to a fairly prosperous husband. So Uncle Ken divided his year among them. Three months with Aunt Ruby in Nainital. Three months with Aunt Susie in Kashmir. Three months with my mother (not quite so affluent) in Jamnagar. And three months in the Vet Hospital in Bareilly, where Aunt Mabel ran the hospital for her veterinary husband. In this way he never overstayed his welcome. A sister can look after a brother for just three months at a time and no more. Uncle K had it worked out to perfection.

But I had no sisters and I couldn't live forever on the royalties of a single novel. So I had to write others. So I came to the hills.

The hillmen go to the plains to make a living. I had to come to the hills to try and make mine.

'Prem,' I said, 'why don't you work for me?'

'And what about my uncle?'

'He seems ready to desert me any day. His grandfather is ill, he says, and he wants to go home.'

'His grandfather died last year.'

'That's what I mean—he's getting restless. And I don't mind if he goes. These days he seems to be suffering from a form of sleeping sickness. I have to get up first and make his tea…'

Sitting here under the cherry tree, whose leaves are just

beginning to turn yellow, I rest my chin on my knees and gaze across the valley to where Prem moves about in the garden. Looking back over the seven years he has been with me, I recall some of the nicest things about him. They come to me in no particular order—just pieces of cinema—coloured slides slipping across the screen of memory...

Prem rocking his infant son to sleep—crooning to him, passing his large hand gently over the child's curly head—Prem following me down to the police station when I was arrested (on a warrant from Bombay, charging me with writing an allegedly obscene short story!), and waiting outside until I reappeared, his smile, when I found him in Delhi, his large, irrepressible laughter, most in evidence when he was seeing an old Laurel and Hardy movie.

Of course, there were times when he could be infuriating, stubborn, deliberately pig-headed, sending me little notes of resignation—but I never found it difficult to overlook these little acts of self-indulgence. He had brought much love and laughter into my life, and what more could a lonely man ask for?

It was his stubborn streak that limited the length of his stay in the headmaster's household. Mr Good was tolerant enough. But Mrs Good was one of those women who, when they are pleased with you, go out of their way to help, pamper and flatter, but when displeased, become vindictive, going out of their way to harm or destroy. Mrs Good sought power—over her husband, her dog, her favourite pupils, her servant... She had absolute power over the husband and the dog, partial power over her slightly bewildered pupils, and none at all over Prem, who missed the subtleties of her designs upon his soul. He did not respond to her mothering, or to the way in which she tweaked him on the cheeks, brushed against him in the kitchen and made admiring remarks about his looks and physique. Memsahibs, he knew, were not for him. So he kept a stony face and went diligently about his duties. And she felt slighted, put in her place. Her liking turned to dislike. Instead of admiring remarks, she began making disparaging remarks about his looks, his clothes, his manners. She found fault with his cooking. No longer was it 'lovely'. She even accused him of taking away the dog's meat and giving it to a poor family living on the hillside—no more heinous crime could be imagined! Mr Good threatened him with dismissal. So Prem became stubborn. The following day he withheld the dog's food altogether, threw it down the khud where it was seized upon by innumerable strays, and went off to the pictures.

That was the end of his job. 'I'll have to go home now,' he told me. 'I won't get another job in this area. The mem will see to that.'

'Stay a few days,' I said.

'I have only enough money with which to get home.'

'Keep it for going home. You can stay with me for a few days, while you look around. Your uncle won't mind sharing his food with you.'

His uncle did mind. He did not like the idea of working for his nephew as well; it seemed to him no part of his duties. And he was apprehensive that Prem might get his job.

So Prem stayed no longer than a week.

Here on the knoll the grass is just beginning to turn October yellow. The first clouds approaching winter cover the sky. The trees are very still. The birds are silent. Only a cricket keeps singing on the oak tree. Perhaps there will be a storm before evening. A storm like the one in which Prem arrived at the cottage with his wife and child—but that's jumping too far ahead...

After he had returned to his village, it was several months before I saw him again. His uncle told me he had taken up a job in Delhi. There was an address. It did not seem complete, but I resolved that when I was next in Delhi I would try to see him.

The opportunity came in May, as the hot winds of summer blew across the plains. It was the time of year when people who can afford it, try to get away to the hills. I dislike New Delhi at the best of times, and I hate it in summer. People compete with each other in being bad-tempered and mean. But I had to go down—I don't remember why, but it must have seemed very necessary at the time—and I took the opportunity to try and see Prem.

Nothing went right for me. Of course the address was all wrong, and I wandered about in a remote, dusty, treeless colony called Vasant Vihar (Spring Garden) for over two hours, asking all the domestic servants I came across if they could put me in touch with Prem Singh of Village Koli, Pauri Garhwal. There were innumerable Prem Singhs, but apparently none who belonged to Village Koli. I returned to my hotel and took two days to recover from heatstroke before returning to Mussoorie, thanking God for mountains!

And then the uncle gave notice. He'd found a better-paid job in Dehradun and was anxious to be off. I didn't try to stop him.

For the next six months I lived in the cottage without any help. I did not find this difficult. I was used to living alone. It wasn't service that I needed but companionship. In the cottage it was very quiet. The ghosts of long-dead residents were sympathetic but unobtrusive. The song of the whistling thrush was beautiful, but I knew he was not singing for me. Up the valley came the sound of a flute, but I never saw the flute player. My affinity was with the little red fox who roamed the hillside below the cottage. I met him one night and wrote these lines:

> As I walked home last night
> I saw a lone fox dancing
> In the cold moonlight.
> I stood and watched—then
> Took the low road, knowing
> the night was his by right.
> Sometimes, when words ring true,
> I'm like a lone fox dancing
> In the morning dew.

During the rains, watching the dripping trees and the mist climbing the valley, I wrote a great deal of poetry. Loneliness is of value to poets. But poetry didn't bring me much money, and funds were low. And then, just as I was wondering if I would have to give up my freedom and take a job again, a publisher bought the paperback rights of one of my children's stories, and I was free to live and write as I pleased—for another three months!

That was in November. To celebrate, I took a long walk through the Landour bazaar and up the Tehri road. It was a good day for walking, and it was dark by the time I returned to the outskirts of the town. Someone stood waiting for me on the road above the cottage. I hurried past him.

> If I am not for myself,
> Who will be for me?

And if I am not for others,
What am I?
And if not now, when?

I startled myself with the memory of these words of Hillel, the ancient Hebrew sage. I walked back to the shadows where the youth stood, and saw that it was Prem.

'Prem!' I said. 'Why are you sitting out here, in the cold? Why did you not go to the house?'

'I went, sir, but there was a lock on the door. I thought you had gone away.'

'And you were going to remain here, on the road?'

'Only for tonight. I would have gone down to Dehra in the morning.'

'Come, let's go home. I have been waiting for you. I looked for you in Delhi, but could not find the place where you were working.'

'I have left them now.'

'And your uncle has left me. So will you work for me now?'

'For as long as you wish.'

'For as long as the gods wish.'

We did not go straight home, but returned to the bazaar and took our meal at the Sindhi Sweet Shop—hot puris and strong sweet tea.

We walked home together in the bright moonlight. I felt sorry for the little fox dancing alone.

That was twenty years ago, and Prem and his wife and three children are still with me. But we live in a different house now, on another hill.

THE LAST TONGA RIDE

It was a warm spring day in Dehra, and the walls of the bungalow were aflame with flowering bougainvillaea. The papayas were ripening. The scent of sweetpeas drifted across the garden. Grandmother sat in an easy chair in a shady corner of the verandah, her knitting needles clicking away, her head nodding now and then. She was knitting a pullover for my father. 'Delhi has cold winters,' she had said, and although the winter was still eight months away, she had set to work on getting our woollens ready.

In the Kathiawar states, touched by the warm waters of the Arabian Sea, it had never been cold but Dehra lies at the foot of the first range of the Himalayas.

Grandmother's hair was white, her eyes were not very strong but her fingers moved quickly with the needles and the needles kept clicking all morning.

When Grandmother wasn't looking, I picked geranium leaves, crushed them between my fingers and pressed them to my nose.

I had been in Dehra with my grandmother for almost a month and I had not seen my father during this time. We had

The Last Tonga Ride

never before been separated for so long. He wrote to me every week, and sent me books and picture postcards, and I would walk to the end of the road to meet the postman as early as possible, to see if there was any mail for us.

We heard the jingle of tonga-bells at the gate, and a familiar horse-buggy came rattling up the drive.

'I'll see who's come,' I said, and ran down the verandah steps and across the garden.

It was Bansi Lal in his tonga. There were many tongas and tonga-drivers in Dehra but Bansi was my favourite driver. He was young and handsome and he always wore a clean white shirt and pyjamas. His pony, too, was bigger and faster than the other tonga ponies. Bansi didn't have a passenger, so I asked him, 'What have you come for, Bansi?'

'Your grandmother sent for me, dost.' He did not call me 'chota sahib' or 'baba', but 'dost' and this made me feel much more important. Not every small boy could boast of a tonga-driver for his friend!

'Where are you going, Granny?' I asked, after I had run back to the verandah.

'I'm going to the bank.'

'Can I come too?'

'Whatever for? What will you do in the bank?'

'Oh, I won't come inside, I'll sit in the tonga with Bansi.'

'Come along, then.'

We helped Grandmother into the back seat of the tonga, and then I joined Bansi in the driver's seat. He said something to his pony, and the pony set off at a brisk trot, out of the gate and down the road.

'Now, not too fast, Bansi,' said Grandmother, who didn't

like anything that went too fast—tonga, motor car, train, or bullock-cart.

'Fast?' said Bansi. 'Have no fear, Memsahib. This pony has never gone fast in its life. Even if a bomb went off behind us, we could go no faster. I have another pony, which I use for racing when customers are in a hurry. This pony is reserved for you, Memsahib.'

There was no other pony, but Grandmother did not know this, and was mollified by the assurance that she was riding in the slowest tonga in Dehra.

A ten-minute ride brought us to the bazaar. Grandmother's bank, the Allahabad Bank, stood near the clock tower. She was gone for about half an hour and during this period Bansi and I sauntered about in front of the shops. The pony had been left with some green stuff to munch.

'Do you have any money on you?' asked Bansi.

'Four annas,' I said.

'Just enough for two cups of tea,' said Bansi, putting his arm round my shoulders and guiding me towards a tea stall. The money passed from my palm to his.

'You can have tea, if you like,' I said. 'I'll have a lemonade.'

'So be it, friend. A tea and a lemonade, and be quick about it,' said Bansi to the boy in the stall and presently the drinks were set before us and Bansi was making a sound rather like his pony when he drank, while I burped my way through some green, gaseous stuff that tasted more like soap than lemonade.

When Grandmother came out of the bank, she looked pensive, and did not talk much during the ride back to the house except to tell me to behave myself when I leaned over to

The Last Tonga Ride

pat the pony on its rump. After paying off Bansi, she marched straight indoors.

'When will you come again?' I asked Bansi.

'When my services are required, dost. I have to make a living, you know. But I tell you what, since we are friends, the next time I am passing this way after leaving a fare, I will jingle my bells at the gate and if you are free and would like a ride—a fast ride—you can join me. It won't cost you anything. Just bring some money for a cup of tea.'

'All right—since we are friends,' I said.

'Since we are friends.'

And touching the pony very lightly with the handle of his whip, he sent the tonga rattling up the drive and out of the gate. I could hear Bansi singing as the pony cantered down the road.

Ayah was waiting for me in the bedroom, her hands resting on her broad hips—sure sign of an approaching storm.

'So you went off to the bazaar without telling me,' she said. (It wasn't enough that I had Grandmother's permission!) 'And all this time I've been waiting to give you your bath.'

'It's too late now, isn't it?' I asked hopefully.

'No, it isn't. There's still an hour left for lunch. Off with your clothes!'

While I undressed, Ayah berated me for keeping the company of tonga-drivers like Bansi. I think she was a little jealous.

'He is a rogue, that man. He drinks, gambles and smokes opium. He has TB and other terrible diseases. So don't you be too friendly with him, understand, baba?'

I nodded my head sagely but said nothing. I thought Ayah was exaggerating, as she always did about people, and besides, I had no intention of giving up free tonga rides.

As my father had told me, Dehra was a good place for trees, and Grandmother's house was surrounded by several kinds—peepul, seem, mango, jackfruit, papaya and an ancient banyan tree. Some of the trees had been planted by my father and grandfather.

'How old is the jackfruit tree?' I asked Grandmother.

'Now let me see,' said Grandmother, looking very thoughtful. 'I should remember the jackfruit tree. Oh yes, your grandfather put it down in 1927. It was during the rainy season. I remember, because it was your father's birthday and we celebrated it by planting a tree. 14 July 1927. Long before you were born!'

The banyan tree grew behind the house. Its spreading branches, which hung to the ground and took root again, formed a number of twisting passageways in which I liked to wander. The tree was older than the house, older than my grandparents, as old as Dehra. I could hide myself in its branches behind thick, green leaves and spy on the world below.

It was an enormous tree, about sixty feet high, and the first time I saw it I trembled with excitement because I had never seen such a marvellous tree before. I approached it slowly, even cautiously, as I wasn't sure the tree wanted my friendship. It looked as though it had many secrets. There were sounds and movement in the branches but I couldn't see who or what made the sounds.

The tree made the first move, the first overture of friendship. It allowed a leaf to fall.

The leaf brushed against my face as it floated down, but before it could reach the ground I caught and held it. I studied the leaf, running my fingers over its smooth, glossy texture. Then I put out my hand and touched the rough bark of the tree and this felt good to me. So I removed my shoes and socks

The Last Tonga Ride

as people do when they enter a holy place, and finding first a foothold and then a handhold on that broad trunk, I pulled myself up with the help of the tree's aerial roots.

As I climbed, it seemed as though someone was helping me; invisible hands, the hands of the spirit in the tree, touched me and helped me climb.

But although the tree wanted me, there were others who were disturbed and alarmed by my arrival. A pair of parrots suddenly shot out of a hole in the trunk and, with shrill cries, flew across the garden—flashes of green and red and gold. A squirrel looked out from behind a branch, saw me, and went scurrying away to inform his friends and relatives.

I climbed higher, looked up, and saw a red beak poised above my head. I shrank away, but the hornbill made no attempt to attack me. He was relaxing in his home, which was a great hole in the tree trunk. Only the bird's head and great beak were showing. He looked at me in a rather bored way, drowsily opening and shutting his eyes.

'So many creatures live here,' I said to myself. 'I hope none of them are dangerous!'

At that moment the hornbill lunged at a passing cricket. Bill and tree trunk met with a loud and resonant 'Tonk!'

I was so startled that I nearly fell out of the tree. But it was a difficult tree to fall out of! It was full of places where one could sit or even lie down. So I moved away from the hornbill, crawled along a branch which had sent out supports, and so moved quite a distance from the main body of the tree. I left its cold, dark depths for an area penetrated by shafts of sunlight.

No one could see me. I lay flat on the broad branch hidden by a screen of leaves. People passed by on the road below. A sahib in a sun-helmet. His memsahib twirling a coloured silk sun-umbrella. Obviously she did not want to get too brown and be mistaken for a country-born person. Behind them, a pram wheeled along by a nanny.

Then there were a number of Indians—some in white dhotis, some in western clothes, some in loincloths. Some with baskets on their heads. Others with coolies to carry their baskets for them.

A cloud of dust, the blare of a horn, and down the road, like an out-of-condition dragon, came the latest Morris touring car. Then cyclists. Then a man with a basket of papayas balanced on his head. Following him, a man with a performing monkey. This man rattled a little hand drum, and children followed the man and the monkey along the road. They stopped in the shade of a mango tree on the other side of the road. The little red monkey wore a frilled dress and a baby's bonnet. It danced for the children, while the man sang and played his drum.

The clip-clop of a tonga pony, and Bansi's tonga came rattling down the road. I called down to him and he reined in with a shout of surprise, and looked up into the branches of the banyan tree.

'What are you doing up there?' he cried.

'Hiding from Grandmother,' I said.

'And when are you coming for that ride?'

'On Tuesday afternoon,' I said.

'Why not today?'

'Ayah won't let me. But she has Tuesdays off.'

Bansi spat red paan juice across the road. 'Your ayah is jealous,' he said.

'I know,' I said. 'Women are always jealous, aren't they? I suppose it's because she doesn't have a tonga.'

The Last Tonga Ride

'It's because she doesn't have a tonga-driver,' said Bansi, grinning up at me. 'Never mind. I'll come on Tuesday—that's the day after tomorrow, isn't it?'

I nodded down to him, and then started backing along my branch, because I could hear Ayah calling in the distance. Bansi leant forward and smacked his pony across the rump, and the tonga shot forward.

'What were you doing up there?' asked Ayah a little later.

'I was watching a snake cross the road,' I said. I knew she couldn't resist talking about snakes. There weren't as many in Dehra as there had been in Kathiawar and she was thrilled that I had seen one.

'Was it moving towards you or away from you?' she asked.

'It was going away.'

Ayah's face clouded over. 'That means poverty for the beholder,' she said gloomily.

Later, while scrubbing me down in the bathroom, she began to air all her prejudices, which included drunkards ('they die quickly anyway'), misers ('they get murdered sooner or later') and tonga-drivers ('they have all the vices').

'You are a very lucky boy,' she said suddenly, peering closely at my tummy.

'Why?' I asked. 'You just said I would be poor because I saw a snake going the wrong way.'

'Well, you won't be poor for long. You have a mole on your tummy, and that's very lucky. And there is one under your armpit, which means you will be famous. Do you have one on the neck? No, thank God! A mole on the neck is the sign of a murderer!'

'Do you have any moles?' I asked.

Ayah nodded seriously, and pulling her sleeve up to her shoulder, showed me a large mole high on her arm.

'What does that mean?' I asked.

'It means a life of great sadness,' said Ayah gloomily.

'Can I touch it?' I asked.

'Yes, touch it,' she said, and taking my hand, she placed it against the mole.

'It's a nice mole,' I said, wanting to make Ayah happy. 'Can I kiss it?'

'You can kiss it,' said Ayah.

I kissed her on the mole.

'That's nice,' she said.

Tuesday afternoon came at last, and as soon as Grandmother was asleep and Ayah had gone to the bazaar, I was at the gate, looking up and down the road for Bansi and his tonga. He was not long in coming. Before the tonga turned into the road, I could hear his voice, singing to the accompaniment of the carriage bells. He reached down, took my hand, and hoisted me on to the seat beside him. Then we went off down the road at a steady jogtrot. It was only when we reached the outskirts of the town that Bansi encouraged his pony to greater efforts. He rose in his seat, leaned forward and slapped the pony across the haunches. From a brisk trot we changed to a carefree canter. The tonga swayed from side to side. I clung to Bansi's free arm, while he grinned at me, his mouth red with paan juice.

'Where shall we go, dost?' he asked.

'Nowhere,' I said. 'Anywhere.'

'We'll go to the river,' said Bansi.

The 'river' was really a swift mountain stream that ran through the forests outside Dehra, joining the Ganga about

The Last Tonga Ride

fifteen miles away. It was almost dry during the winter and early summer; in flood during the monsoon.

The road out of Dehra was a gentle decline and soon we were rushing headlong through the tea gardens and eucalyptus forests, the pony's hoofs striking sparks off the metalled road, the carriage wheels groaning and creaking so loudly that I feared one of them would come off and that we would all be thrown into a ditch or into the small canal that ran beside the road. We swept through mango groves, through guava and litchi orchards, past broad-leaved sal and shisham trees. Once in the sal forest, Bansi turned the tonga on to a rough cart track, and we continued along it for about a furlong, until the road dipped down to the stream bed.

'Let us go straight into the water,' said Bansi. 'You and I and the pony!' And he drove the tonga straight into the middle of the stream, where the water came up to the pony's knees.

'I am not a great one for baths,' said Bansi, 'but the pony needs one, and why should a horse smell sweeter than its owner?' Saying which, he flung off his clothes and jumped into the water.

'Better than bathing under a tap!' he cried, slapping himself on the chest and thighs. 'Come down, dost, and join me!'

After some hesitation I joined him, but had some difficulty in keeping on my feet in the fast current. I grabbed at the pony's tail, and hung on to it, while Bansi began sloshing water over the patient animal's back.

After this, Bansi led both me and the pony out of the stream and together we gave the carriage a good washing down. I'd had a free ride and Bansi got the services of a free helper for the long overdue spring cleaning of his tonga. After we had finished the job, he presented me with a packet of aam pafiat—a sticky toffee made from mango pulp—and for some time I tore at it as a dog tears at a bit of old leather. Then I felt drowsy and lay down on the brown, sun-warmed grass. Crickets and grasshoppers were telephoning each other from tree and bush and a pair of bluejays rolled, dived and swooped acrobatically overhead.

Bansi had no watch. He looked at the sun and said, 'It is past three. When will that ayah of yours be home? She is more frightening than your grandmother!'

'She comes at four.'

'Then we must hurry back. And don't tell her where we've been, or I'll never be able to come to your house again. Your grandmother's one of my best customers.'

'That means you'd be sorry if she died.'

'I would indeed, my friend.'

Bansi raced the tonga back to town. There was very little motor traffic in those days, and tongas and bullock-carts were far more numerous than they are today.

We were back five minutes before Ayah returned. Before Bansi left, he promised to take me for another ride the following week.

◆

The house in Dehra had to be sold. My father had not left any money; he had never realized that his health would deteriorate so rapidly from the malarial fevers which had grown in frequency; he was still planning for the future when he died. Now that my father had gone, Grandmother saw no point in staying on in India; there was nothing left in the bank and she needed money for our passages to England, so the house had to go. Dr Ghose, who had a thriving medical practice in Dehra, made

The Last Tonga Ride

her a reasonable offer, which she accepted.

Then things happened very quickly. Grandmother sold most of our belongings, because as she said, we wouldn't he able to cope with a lot of luggage. The kabaris came in droves, buying our crockery, furniture, carpets and clocks at throwaway prices. Grandmother hated parting with some of her possessions, such as the carved giltwood mirror, her walnut-wood armchair and her rosewood writing desk, but it was impossible to take them with us. They were carried away in a bullock-cart.

Ayah was very unhappy at first but cheered up when Grandmother got her a job with a tea-planter's family in Assam. It was arranged that she could stay with us until we left Dehra.

We left at the end of September, just as the monsoon clouds broke up, scattered, and were driven away by soft breezes from the Himalayas. There was no time to revisit the island where my father and I had planted our trees. And in the urgency and excitement of the preparations for our departure, I forgot to recover my small treasures from the hole in the banyan tree. It was only when we were in Bansi's tonga, on the way to the station, that I remembered my top, catapult and Iron Cross. Too late! To go back for them would mean missing the train.

'Hurry!' urged Grandmother nervously. 'We mustn't be late for the train, Bansi.'

Bansi flicked the reins and shouted to his pony, and for once in her life Grandmother submitted to being carried along the road at a brisk trot.

'It's five to nine,' she said, 'and the train leaves at nine.'

'Do not worry, Memsahib. I have been taking you to the station for fifteen years, and you have never missed a train!'

'No,' said Grandmother. 'And I don't suppose you'll ever

take me to the station again, Bansi.'

'Times are changing, Memsahib. Do you know that there is now a taxi—a *motor car*—competing with the tongas of Dehra? You are lucky to be leaving. If you stay, you will see me starve to death!'

'We will all starve to death if we don't catch that train,' said Grandmother.

'Do not worry about the train, it never leaves on time, and no one expects it to. If it left at nine o' clock, everyone would miss it.'

Bansi was right. We arrived at the station at five minutes past nine, and rushed on to the platform, only to find that the train had not yet arrived.

The platform was crowded with people waiting to catch the same train or to meet people arriving on it. Ayah was there already, standing guard over a pile of miscellaneous luggage. We sat down on our boxes and became part of the platform life at an Indian railway station.

Moving among piles of bedding and luggage were sweating, cursing coolies; vendors of magazines, sweetmeats, tea and betel-leaf preparations; also stray dogs, stray people and sometimes a stray stationmaster. The cries of the vendors mixed with the general clamour of the station and the shunting of a steam engine in the yards. 'Tea, hot tea!' Sweets, papads, hot stuff, cold drinks, toothpowder, pictures of film stars, bananas, balloons, wooden toys, clay images of the gods. The platform had become a bazaar.

Ayah was giving me all sorts of warnings.

'Remember, baba, don't lean out of the window when the train is moving. There was that American boy who lost his head last year! And don't eat rubbish at every station between here and Bombay. And see that no strangers enter the compartment. Mr Wilkins was murdered *and* robbed last year!'

The station bell clanged, and in the distance there appeared a big, puffing steam engine, painted green and gold and black. A stray dog, with a lifetime's experience of trains, darted away across the railway lines. As the train came alongside the platform, doors opened, window shutters fell, faces appeared in the openings, and even before the train had come to a stop, people were trying to get in or out.

For a few moments there was chaos. The crowd surged backward and forward. No one could get out. No one could get in. A hundred people were leaving the train, two hundred were getting into it. No one wanted to give way.

The problem was solved by a man climbing out of a window. Others followed his example and the pressure at the doors eased and people started squeezing into their compartments.

Grandmother had taken the precaution of reserving berths in a first-class compartment, and assisted by Bansi and half a dozen coolies, we were soon inside with all our luggage. A whistle blasted and we were off! Bansi had to jump from the running train.

As the engine gathered speed, I ignored Ayah's advice and put my head out of the window to look back at the receding platform. Ayah and Bansi were standing on the platform, waving to me and I kept waving to them until the train rushed into the darkness and the bright lights of Dehra were swallowed up in the night. New lights, dim and flickering came into existence as we passed small villages. The stars too were visible and I saw a shooting star streaking through the heavens.

I remembered something that Ayah had once told me,

that stars are the spirits of good men, and I wondered if that shooting star was a sign from my father that he was aware of our departure and would be with us on our journey. And I remembered something else that Ayah had said—that if one wished on a shooting star, one's wish would be granted, provided of course that one thrust all five fingers into the mouth at the same time!

'What on earth are you doing?' asked Grandmother staring at me as I thrust my hand into my mouth.

'Making a wish,' I said.

'Oh,' said Grandmother.

She was preoccupied, and didn't ask me what I was wishing for; nor did I tell her.

THE CROOKED TREE

You must pass your exams and go to college, but do not feel that if you fail, you will be able to do nothing.

My room in Shahganj was very small. I had paced about in it so often that I knew its exact measurements: twelve feet by ten. The string of my cot needed tightening. The dip in the middle was so pronounced that I invariably woke up in the morning with a backache, but I was hopeless at tightening charpoy strings.

Under the cot was my tin trunk. Its contents ranged from old, rejected manuscripts to clothes and letters and photographs. I had resolved that one day, when I had made some money with a book, I would throw the trunk and everything else out of the window, and leave Shahganj forever. But until then I was a prisoner. The rent was nominal, the window had a view of the bus stop and rickshaw stand, and I had nowhere else to go.

I did not live entirely alone. Sometimes a beggar spent the night on the balcony, and, during cold or wet weather, the boys from the tea shop, who normally slept on the pavement, crowded into the room.

Usually I woke early in the mornings, as sleep was fitful, uneasy, crowded with dreams. I knew it was five o'clock when I heard the first upcountry bus leaving its shed. I would then get up and take a walk in the fields beyond the railroad tracks.

One morning, while I was walking in the fields, I noticed someone lying across the pathway, his head and shoulders hidden by the stalks of young sugar cane. When I came near, I saw he was a boy of about sixteen. His body was twitching convulsively, his face was very white, except where a little blood had trickled down his chin. His legs kept moving and his hands fluttered restlessly, helplessly.

'What's the matter with you?' I asked, kneeling down beside him.

But he was still unconscious and could not answer me.

I ran down the footpath to a well and, dipping the end of my shirt in a shallow trough of water, ran back and sponged the boy's face. The twitching ceased and, though he still breathed heavily, his hands became still and his face calm. He opened his eyes and stared at me without any immediate comprehension.

'You have bitten your tongue,' I said, wiping the blood from his mouth. 'Don't worry. I'll stay with you until you feel better.'

He sat up now and said, 'I'm all right, thank you.'

'What happened?' I asked, sitting down beside him.

'Oh, nothing much. It often happens, I don't know why. But I cannot control it.'

'Have you seen a doctor?'

'I went to the hospital in the beginning. They gave me some pills, which I had to take every day. But the pills made me so tired and sleepy that I couldn't work properly. So I stopped taking them. Now this happens once or twice a month. But what does it matter? I'm all right when it's over, and I don't feel anything while it is happening.'

He got to his feet, dusting his clothes and smiling at me. He was slim, long-limbed and bony. There was a little fluff on his cheeks and the promise of a moustache.

'Where do you live?' I asked. 'I'll walk back with you.'

'I don't live anywhere,' he said. 'Sometimes I sleep in the temple, sometimes in the gurdwara. In summer months I sleep in the municipal gardens.'

'Well, then let me come with you as far as the gardens.'

He told me that his name was Kamal, that he studied at the Shahganj High School, and that he hoped to pass his examinations in a few months' time. He was studying hard and, if he passed with a good division, he hoped to attend a college. If he failed, there was only the prospect of continuing to live in the municipal gardens...

He carried with him a small tray of merchandise, supported by straps that went round his shoulders. In it were combs and buttons and cheap toys and little vials of perfume. All day he walked about Shahganj, selling odds and ends to people in the bazaar or at their houses. He made, on an average, two rupees a day, which was enough for his food and his school fees.

He told me all this while we walked back to the bus stand. I returned to my room, to try and write something, while Kamal went on to the bazaar to try and sell his wares.

There was nothing very unusual about Kamal's being an orphan and a refugee. During the communal holocaust of 1947, thousands of homes had been broken up, and women and children had been killed. What was unusual in Kamal was his sensitivity, a quality I thought rare in a Punjabi youth who had grown up in the Frontier Provinces during a period of hate and violence. And it was not so much his positive attitude to life that appealed to me (most people in Shahganj were completely resigned to their lot) as his gentleness, his quiet voice and the smile that flickered across his face regardless of whether he was sad or happy. In the morning, when I opened my door, I found Kamal asleep at the top of the steps. His tray lay a few feet away. I shook him gently, and he woke at once.

'Have you been sleeping here all night?' I asked. 'Why didn't you come inside?'

'It was very late,' he said. 'I didn't want to disturb you.'

'Someone could have stolen your things while you slept.'

'Oh, I sleep quite lightly. Besides, I have nothing of special value. But I came to ask you something.'

'Do you need any money?'

'No. I want you to take your meal with me tonight.'

'But where? You don't have a place of your own. It will be too expensive in a restaurant.'

'In your room,' said Kamal. 'I will bring the food and cook it here. You have a stove?'

'I think so,' I said. 'I will have to look for it.'

'I will come at seven,' said Kamal, strapping on his tray. 'Don't worry. I know how to cook!'

He ran down the steps and made for the bazaar. I began to look for the oil stove, found it at the bottom of my tin trunk, and then discovered I hadn't any pots or pans or dishes. Finally, I borrowed these from Deep Chand, the barber.

Kamal brought a chicken for our dinner. This was a costly

luxury in Shahganj, to be taken only two or three times a year. He had bought the bird for three rupees, which was cheap, considering it was not too skinny. While Kamal set about roasting it, I went down to the bazaar and procured a bottle of beer on credit, and this served as an appetizer.

'We are having an expensive meal,' I observed. 'Three rupees for the chicken and three rupees for the beer. But I wish we could do it more often.'

'We should do it at least once a month,' said Kamal. 'It should be possible if we work hard.'

'You know how to work. You work from morning to night.'

'But you are a writer, Rusty. That is different. You have to wait for a mood.'

'Oh, I'm not a genius that I can afford the luxury of moods. No, I'm just lazy, that's all.'

'Perhaps you are writing the wrong things.'

'I know I am. But I don't know how I can write anything else.'

'Have you tried?'

'Yes, but there is no money in it. I wish I could make a living in some other way. Even if I repaired cycles, I would make more money.'

'Then why not repair cycles?'

'No, I will not repair cycles. I would rather be a bad writer than a good repairer of cycles. But let us not think of work. There is time enough for work. I want to know more about you.'

Kamal did not know if his parents were alive or dead. He had lost them, literally, when he was six. It happened at the Amritsar railroad station, where trains coming across the border disgorged thousands of refugees, or pulled into the station half empty, drenched with blood and littered with corpses.

Kamal and his parents were lucky to escape the massacre. Had they travelled on an earlier train (they had tried desperately to get into one), they might well have been killed, but circumstances favoured them then, only to trick them later.

Kamal was clinging to his mother's sari, while she remained close to her husband, who was elbowing his way through the frightened, bewildered throng of refugees. Glancing over his shoulder at a woman who lay on the ground, wailing and beating her breasts, Kamal collided with a burly Sikh and lost his grip on his mother's sari.

The Sikh had a long curved sword at his waist, and Kamal stared up at him in awe and fascination—at his long hair, which had fallen loose, and his wild black beard, and the bloodstains on his white shirt. The Sikh pushed him out of the way and when Kamal looked around for his mother, she was not to be seen. She was hidden from him by a mass of restless bodies, pushed in different directions. He could hear her calling, 'Kamal, where are you, Kamal?' He tried to force his way through the crowd, in the direction of the voice, but he was carried the other way...

At night, when the platform was empty, he was still searching for his mother. Eventually, some soldiers took him away. They looked for his parents, but without success, and finally, they sent Kamal to a refugee camp. From there he went to an orphanage. But when he was eight, and felt himself a man, he ran away.

He worked for some time as a helper in a tea shop, but, when he started getting epileptic fits, the shopkeeper asked him to leave, and he found himself on the streets, begging for a living. He begged for a year, moving from one town to another, and ended up finally at Shahganj. By then he was twelve and too old to beg, but he had saved some money, and with it he bought a small stock of combs, buttons, cheap perfumes and bangles, and, converting himself into a mobile shop, went from door to door, selling his wares.

Shahganj was a small town, and there was no house that Kamal hadn't visited. Everyone recognized him, and there were some who offered him food and drink; the children knew him well, because he played a small flute whenever he made his rounds, and they followed him to listen to the flute.

I began to look forward to Kamal's presence. He dispelled some of my own loneliness. I found I could work better, knowing that I did not have to work alone. And Kamal came to me, perhaps because I was the first person to have taken a personal interest in his life, and because I saw nothing frightening in his sickness. Most people in Shahganj thought epilepsy was infectious; some considered it a form of divine punishment for sins committed in a former life. Except for children, those who knew of his condition generally gave him a wide berth.

At sixteen, a boy grows like young wheat, springing up so fast that he is unaware of what is taking place within him. His mind quickens, his gestures become more confident. Hair sprouts like young grass on his face and chest, and his muscles begin to mature. Never again will he experience so much change and growth in so short a time. He is full of currents and countercurrents.

Kamal combined the bloom of youth with the beauty of the short-lived. It made me sad even to look at his pale, slim body. It hurt me to look into his eyes. Life and death were always struggling in their depths.

'Should I go to Delhi and take up a job?' I asked.

'Why not? You are always talking about it.'

'Why don't you come, too? Perhaps they can stop your fits.'

'We will need money for that. When I have passed my examinations, I will come.'

'Then I will wait,' I said. I was twenty-two, and there was world enough and time for everything.

We decided to save a little money from his small earnings and my occasional payments. We would need money to go to Delhi, money to live there until we could earn a living. We put away twenty rupees one week, but lost it the next when we lent it to a friend who owned a cycle rickshaw. But this gave us the occasional use of his cycle rickshaw, and early one morning, with Kamal sitting on the crossbar, I rode out of Shahganj.

After cycling for about two miles, we got down and pushed the cycle off the road, taking a path through a paddy field and then through a field of young maize, until in the distance we saw a tree, a crooked tree, growing beside an old well.

I do not know the name of that tree. I had never seen one like it before. It had a crooked trunk and crooked branches, and was clothed in thick, broad, crooked leaves, like the leaves on which food is served in the bazaar.

In the trunk of the tree there was a hole, and when we set the bicycle down with a crash, a pair of green parrots flew out, and went dipping and swerving across the fields. There was grass around the well, cropped short by grazing cattle.

We sat in the shade of the crooked tree, and Kamal untied the red cloth in which he had brought our food. When we had eaten, we stretched ourselves out on the grass. I closed my eyes and became aware of a score of different sensations. I heard a cricket singing in the tree, the cooing of pigeons from the walls of the old well, the quiet breathing of Kamal, the parrots returning to the tree, the distant hum of an airplane. I smelled the grass and the old bricks round the well and the promise of rain. I felt Kamal's fingers against my arm, and the sun creeping over my cheek. And when I opened my eyes, there were clouds on the horizon, and Kamal was asleep, his arm thrown across his face to keep out the glare.

I went to the well, and putting my shoulders to the ancient handle, turned the wheel, moving it around while cool, clean water gushed out over the stones and along the channel to the fields. The discovery that I could water a field, that I had the power to make things grow, gave me a thrill of satisfaction; it was like writing a story that had the ring of truth. I drank from one of the trays; the water was sweet with age.

Kamal was sitting up, looking at the sky.

'It's going to rain,' he said.

We began cycling homeward, but we were still some way out of Shahganj when it began to rain. A lashing wind swept the rain across our faces, but we exulted in it, and sang at the top of our voices until we reached the Shahganj bus stop.

Across the railroad tracks and the dry riverbed, fields of maize stretched away, until there came a dry region of thorn bushes and lantana scrub, where the earth was cut into jagged cracks, like a jigsaw puzzle. Dotting the landscape were old, abandoned brick kilns. When it rained heavily, the hollows filled up with water.

Kamal and I came to one of these hollows to bathe and swim. There was an island in the middle of it, and on this small mound lay the ruins of a hut where a nightwatchman had once lived, looking after the brick kilns. We would swim out to the island, which was only a few yards from the banks of the hollow. There was a grassy patch in front of the hut, and early in the mornings, before it got too hot, we would wrestle on the grass.

Though I was heavier than Kamal, my chest as sound as a new drum, he had strong, wiry arms and legs, and would often pinion me around the waist with his bony knees. Now, while we wrestled on the new monsoon grass, I felt his body go tense. He stiffened, his legs jerked against my body, and a shudder passed through him. I knew that he had a fit coming on, but I was unable to extricate myself from his arms.

He gripped me more tightly as the fit took possession of him. Instead of struggling, I lay still, tried to absorb some of his anguish, tried to draw some of his agitation to myself. I had a strange fancy that by identifying myself with his convulsions, I might alleviate them.

I pressed against Kamal, and whispered soothingly into his ear, and then, when I noticed his mouth working, I thrust my fingers between his teeth to prevent him from biting his tongue. But so violent was the convulsion that his teeth bit into the flesh of my palm and ground against my knuckles. I shouted with the pain and tried to jerk my hand away, but it was impossible to loosen the grip of his jaws. So I closed my eyes and counted—counted till seven—until consciousness returned to him and his muscles relaxed.

My hand was shaking and covered with blood. I bound it in my handkerchief and kept it hidden from Kamal.

We walked back to the room without talking much. Kamal looked depressed and weak. I kept my hand beneath my shirt, and Kamal was too dejected to notice anything. It was only at night, when he returned from his classes, that he noticed the

The Crooked Tree

cuts, and I told him I had slipped in the road, cutting my hand on some broken glass.

Rain upon Shahganj. And, until the rain stops, Shahganj is fresh and clean and alive. The children run out of their houses, glorying in their nakedness. The gutters choke, and the narrow street becomes a torrent of water, coursing merrily down to the bus stop. It swirls over the trees and the roofs of the town, and the parched earth soaks it up, exuding a fragrance that comes only once in a year, the fragrance of quenched earth, that most exhilarating of smells.

The rain swept in through the door and soaked the cot. When I had succeeded in closing the door, I found the roof leaking, the water trickling down the walls and forming new pictures on the cracking plaster. The door flew open again, and there was Kamal standing on the threshold, shaking himself like a wet dog. Coming in, he stripped and dried himself, and then sat shivering on the bed while I made frantic efforts to close the door again.

'You need some tea,' I said.

He nodded, forgetting to smile for once, and I knew his mind was elsewhere, in one of a hundred possible places from his dreams.

'One day I will write a book,' I said, as we drank strong tea in the fast-fading twilight. 'A real book, about real people. Perhaps it will be about you and me and Shahganj. And then we will run away from Shahganj, fly on the wings of Garuda, and all our troubles will be over and fresh troubles will begin. Why should we mind difficulties, as long as they are new difficulties?'

'First I must pass my exams,' said Kamal. 'Otherwise, I can do nothing, go nowhere.'

'Don't take exams too seriously. I know that in India they

are the passport to any kind of job, and that you cannot become a clerk unless you have a degree. But do not forget that you are studying for the sake of acquiring knowledge, and not for the sake of becoming a clerk. You don't want to become a clerk or a bus conductor, do you? You must pass your exams and go to college, but do not feel that if you fail, you will be able to do nothing. Why, you can start making your own buttons instead of selling other people's!'

'You are right,' said Kamal. 'But why not be an educated button manufacturer?'

'Why not, indeed? That's just what I mean. And, while you are studying for your exams, I will be writing my book. I will start tonight! It is an auspicious night, the beginning of the monsoon.'

The light did not come on. A tree must have fallen across the wires. I lit a candle and placed it on the windowsill and, while the candle spluttered in the steamy air, Kamal opened his books and, with one hand on a book and the other hand playing with his toes—this attitude helped him to concentrate—he devoted his attention to algebra.

I took an ink bottle down from a shelf and, finding it empty, added a little rainwater to the crusted contents. Then I sat down beside Kamal and began to write, but the pen was useless and made blotches all over the paper, and I had no idea what I should write about, though I was full of writing just then. So I began to look at Kamal instead, at his eyes, hidden in shadow, and his hands, quiet in the candlelight, and I followed his breathing and the slight movement of his lips as he read softly to himself.

And, instead of starting my book, I sat and watched Kamal.

Sometimes Kamal played the flute at night, while I was lying awake, and, even when I was asleep, the flute would play in my dreams. Sometimes he brought it to the crooked tree, and played it for the benefit of the birds, but the parrots only made harsh noises and flew away.

Once, when Kamal was playing his flute to a group of children, he had a fit. The flute fell from his hands, and he began to roll about in the dust on the roadside. The children were frightened and ran away. But the next time they heard Kamal play his flute, they came to listen as usual.

That Kamal was gaining in strength I knew from the way he was able to pin me down whenever we wrestled on the grass near the old brick kilns. It was no longer necessary for me to yield deliberately to him. And, though his fits still recurred from time to time—as we knew they would continue to do—he was not so depressed afterwards. The anxiety and the death had gone from his eyes.

His examinations were nearing, and he was working hard. (I had yet to begin the first chapter of my book.) Because of the necessity of selling two or three rupees' worth of articles every day, he did not get much time for studying, but he stuck to his books until past midnight, and it was seldom that I heard his flute.

He put aside his tray of odds and ends during the examinations, and walked to the examination centre instead. And after two weeks, when it was all over, he took up his tray and began his rounds again. In a burst of creativity, I wrote three pages of my novel.

On the morning the results of the examination were due, I rose early, before Kamal, and went down to the news agency. It was five o'clock and the newspapers had just arrived. I went through the columns relating to Shahganj, but I couldn't find Kamal's roll number on the list of successful candidates. I had the number written down on a slip of paper, and I looked at it again to make sure that I had compared it correctly with the others; then I went through the newspaper once more.

When I returned to the room, Kamal was sitting on the doorstep. I didn't have to tell him he had failed. He knew by the look on my face. I sat down beside him, and we said nothing for some time.

'Never mind,' said Kamal, eventually. 'I will pass next year.'

I realized that I was more depressed than he was, and that he was trying to console me.

'If only you'd had more time,' I said.

'I have plenty of time now. Another year. And you will have time in which to finish your book; then we can both go away. Another year of Shahganj won't be so bad. As long as I have your friendship, almost everything else can be tolerated, even my sickness.'

And then, turning to me with an expression of intense happiness, he said, 'Yesterday I was sad, and tomorrow I may be sad again, but today I know that I am happy. I want to live on and on. I feel that life isn't long enough to satisfy me.'

He stood up, the tray hanging from his shoulders.

'What would you like to buy?' he said. 'I have everything you need.'

At the bottom of the steps he turned and smiled at me, and I knew then that I had written my story.